ASCENT

ASCENT

ROLAND SMITH

HOUGHTON MIFFLIN HARCOURT
BOSTON NEW YORK

hmhco.com

The text was set in Plantin Std and Museo Sans

Library of Congress Cataloging-in-Publication Data
Names: Smith, Roland, 1951– author.
Title: Ascent / Roland Smith.
Description: Boston : HMH Books for Young Readers, 2018. |
Series: A Peak Marcello adventure | Summary: Fifteen-year-old Peak Marcello is invited to climb Hkakabo Razi, one of the most isolated mountains in the world, but getting there involves a four-week trek through a tropical rainforest that is rife with hazards, which turns out to be more dangerous than summiting the mountain itself.
Identifiers: LCCN 2017059748 (print) | LCCN 2017046683 (ebook) |
ISBN 9781328830265 (ebook) | ISBN 9780544867598 (hardback)
Subjects: | CYAC: Mountaineering—Fiction. | Survival—Fiction. | Rain forests—Fiction. | Hkakabo Razi (Burma)—Fiction. | Burma—Fiction. | Adventure and adventurers—Fiction. | BISAC: JUVENILE FICTION / Action & Adventure / Survival Stories. | JUVENILE FICTION / Nature & the Natural World / Environment. | JUVENILE FICTION / People & Places / Asia. | JUVENILE FICTION / Boys & Men.
Classification: LCC PZ7.S65766 (print) | LCC PZ7.S65766 As 2018 (ebook) |
DDC [Fic]—dc23
LC record available at https://lccn.loc.gov/2017059748

Printed in the United States of America
DOC 10 9 8 7 6 5 4 3 2 1
4500705766

For Julia Richardson, Elizabeth Bewley, and Lily Kessinger,
my three fabulous editors on the ascent

PART

ONE

The Tangle

ONE

This morning Lwin killed an owl with his slingshot and ate it.

He didn't bother plucking or gutting the bird. He threw it on the coals with its beak, talons, feathers, and large golden eyes, whole, flipped it once with a stick, then consumed it. He offered to share it with me. I told him that I was full after eating my mildewed energy bar, which he didn't understand. Lwin does not speak English. I don't speak Burmese.

Alessia speaks a little Burmese and can communicate with Lwin, after a fashion, but she was in her tent shivering with malaria and missed the owl-over-easy meal.

Lucky for her.

Ethan took off two hours ago, at dawn, for the nearest village to find a doctor, which is a three-hour trek through the rainforest, the jungle, or as I call it, the tangle.

We trudged through the village yesterday. It wasn't much of a village. Seven stilted bamboo huts. Beneath the huts were a couple emaciated dogs, a pig, and six bedraggled chickens, which Lwin eyed hungrily from atop his elephant, Nagathan, who has to be the nastiest elephant that ever walked the earth. The people inside the huts did not venture outside to greet us, or ask who we were, where we were going, or why we were going, like every other villager in every village we've walked through the past seven days, or maybe it's been eight days. I've kind of lost track of time, with every day being as miserable as the previous day. My point is, there will not be a doctor at the village. There isn't a doctor within two hundred miles of here.

I don't think Ethan took the long trek back to the village to find a doctor. I think he went there because he is almost incapable of staying still. He's like a shark. If he doesn't move, he will drown.

Alessia will live. Her fever broke an hour after Ethan left to fetch the phantom doctor. I spent the night by her side listening to her wild hallucinations in a combination of French and English, which I won't share here, or anywhere for as long as I live. I liked her a lot before the malaria attack. I like her even more after having listened to her unleashed ravings. Alessia has a wild side that I don't think she is even aware of. I thought I was going to lose her for a while. Those were the worst moments of my life. I'm not sure that I'm in love, but when I'm with her, I feel anchored. When I'm away from her, I feel adrift. I guess I am in love with her. And I think that she feels the same way about me.

This is the first time I've had a chance to write in this journal since I arrived in Burma. The two Peas, Patrice and Paula, my twin half sisters, nine years old, gave this journal to me at the airport in New York. I didn't tell them that I already had a journal in my back-pack. The one I had picked had swollen to the size of a dictionary in the saturated air. The journal the Peas picked has waterproof pages, which is perfect for the humid jungle.

Mom's last words when I got out of the car at the airport were

"At least there are no alpine peaks in Burma."

I didn't think there were either. It turns out we were both wrong.

Lwin just said something to me, which I couldn't understand, then disappeared into the green tangle to either relieve himself or kill a little animal with his deadly slingshot. We've been with him for over a week. In that time, I've never seen him miss. When the rubber goes back, something dies. He carries his projectiles (steel ball bearings, I think) in a little pouch strapped around his *longyi*, which is a brightly colored tube of cotton cloth. Lwin's *longyi* is especially garish. Red with bright yellow snakelike squiggles on it. Most all Burmese wear these skirts, knotting the *longyi*s around their waists. *Longyi*s are practical attire in the jungle. They are light and cool and take up virtually no space in a bag or a pack. They can be washed in a stream and dried in the sun within a few minutes. Well, not totally dried. Nothing really dries out here.

Ethan started wearing a *longyi* as soon as we left Yangon on the train. Alessia donned a *longyi* three days out, and looks a lot better in one than Ethan does. I'm still wearing my nylon pants and T-shirts in the ridiculous belief that they will protect me from biting insects. My entire body is one big bite. Many of the bites are infected and have turned into weeping sores, which will no doubt leave lifelong scars. Both Ethan and Alessia have begged me to switch to a *longyi*. They have as many bug bites as I do, maybe more, but their logic is that they are cooler while being slowly eaten to death. "Peak, give yourself over to the little Asia skirt. You will be happier," Alessia said in her sweet French accent. So far I have stuck to my T's and *pantalons*. (I've been taking French at school for a year.) I would rather itch in pants than itch in a skirt.

A minute ago, a glob of stinking black ooze hit my chin and

neck. Some of it got into my mouth. I spat it out, cursing Lwin's elephant, Nagathan, who is always flipping crap at us with his gigantic and agile trunk. He's as good with his trunk as Lwin is with his slingshot. I used to love elephants until I met the murderous Nagathan.

Elephants are Burma's four-legged loggers. They are trained almost from birth to harvest trees from Burma's vast teak forests. Teak is one of the country's most valuable exports, along with rubies—and opium. A timber elephant lives its long life deep in the forest with its human handler, or oozie. All of this was explained to me by Ethan, who seems to know everything there is to know about Burma, except for the language and where we are. I forgot to mention that we have been lost for several days.

Back to Nagathan . . .

He's what's known as an iron bell. A dangerous elephant.

When it becomes too hot to work in the timber camps, the oozies set their elephants free in the forest to forage for the night. The following morning, the oozies wake up at dawn, eat a simple breakfast of rice and green tea, then wander into the forest to find their elephants. The oozies find their elephants by listening for their elephants' bells. The oozies make the bells out of teak. Each one has a different tone, and the oozie knows what his elephant's bell sounds like.

Nagathan wears an iron bell around his thick neck, which sets him apart from the other timber elephants. The sound of the iron bell is a warning that a potentially aggressive elephant is in the area. According to Lwin, via Alessia, Nagathan has killed three people; two of them were oozies. The third victim was a young woman who had wandered out of the elephant camp into the forest early one morning and ran across the foraging Nagathan.

Lwin claims that the military was going to execute Nagathan, which Alessia did not believe. She didn't challenge him on his story, but she told me later that she knew of timber elephants who had killed a half dozen people and were still working in the forest. "Timber elephants are worth much more than the drivers on their backs," she said. The government owns most of the timber elephants. Lwin said he talked the military into giving Nagathan to him under the condition he take Nagathan upcountry where he could no longer harm the teak workers. Ethan thinks that Lwin got sick of working hard in the forest for ten dollars a month and decided to go into business for himself by turning his logging truck into a transport truck.

Nagathan threw a second trunkful of rot at me just now—it missed. The stinking glob hit the tree to my right. He might be thirsty. Or maybe he's bored. Lwin has him cross tied between two giant trees. There's a stout rope around his right front ankle and another around his left rear ankle. At first I thought Lwin did this because he didn't want to take the time to find him every morning when we broke camp. But Ethan thinks Lwin ties him up so he doesn't kill us in our tents while we're sleeping.

Nagathan appears to have fallen head over heels, or trunk over tail, for Alessia. Can't say I blame him. Everyone does. Nagathan never throws muck at her. Aside from Lwin, Alessia is the only person Nagathan allows on his back. Ethan and I have to walk, and keep our distance so he doesn't try to whack us. I think Lwin has a huge crush on Alessia as well. Before she came down with her fever, he stayed within whispering distance of her every step we took through the jungle. We keep a close eye on him, making sure he's never alone with her. We'd like to ditch him, but then we'd be stuck with three hundred pounds of gear and no way to haul it.

For now we're stuck with his leering at Alessia and his mumbling to himself when he thinks we can't hear him.

The past couple of days, Alessia has been on elephant back, but yesterday she became too weak to even ride, which is why we had to stop in this little patch of paradise. After we got her into her tent, Lwin wanted to crawl inside to take care of her. Fat chance of that happening. When we told him, he threw a hissy fit about it. We don't know what he said, but as a precaution, I put my tent two inches from hers just in case he tried to slither in at night.

Great. Nagathan tossed yet another clot of stink at me. It missed, but not by much. I think he's trying to get me to move just for the fun of it. I'm not giving in. I'm sitting in the coolest spot in camp. I'm sweating. My clothes look like I took a shower in them. If I move I might melt.

Lwin walked back into camp with a bucket of water in his right hand and a large dead snake draped over his left shoulder. Lwin was smiling. He dumped the snake on the smoking fire, which was too small to accommodate it. I'd say about one fifth of the snake was cooking. Lwin nudged a little more of the body onto the hot embers with his sandaled foot, then walked over to Nagathan and held the bucket up for him to drink from.

This is how he always waters Nagathan. I'm not sure if he does this because he's afraid Nagathan will smash his only bucket, or if he's reminding Nagathan of who's in charge.

The cooking snake started to squirm and sizzle on the coals as if it was still alive. Lwin walked over to the fire and prodded it with his *panga*—a short knife he carries on the rope around his *longyi* opposite his slingshot and elephant hook. He gave me a big orange-toothed grin. It seems everyone in the tangle chews betel nut—men, women, even children. Betel nuts come from the areca palm. The nut is wrapped in a leaf smeared with lime to cause salivation. Ethan, Alessia, and I tried it. It made us dizzy and a little sick to our stomachs. Another downside to the mild narcotic? It turns your teeth permanently orange after long-term use.

Lwin pointed at the snake and made an eating motion with his hand. He was either still hungry after eating the owl, or he had killed the snake and grilled it for me, thinking that I preferred snake flesh over owl flesh.

I did not want to eat a snake for breakfast. Or at any other meal. Ethan would have eaten the snake. He probably would have taken a bite of the owl too. Ethan's two best skills are adaptability and optimism. Alessia would not have eaten the owl or the snake, but she would have refused in such a charming way that Lwin would remember later that she had consumed both animals whole.

Lwin pointed at my pocket. I glanced down, and to my disappointment, saw that I'd left my spoon there from last night's dinner. I wondered if this was why he had slaughtered the owl and the snake. If you have a spoon in your shirt pocket, you must be hungry. Right? Ethan carries a special spoon in his pocket too.

The scaly skin burst when I touched it with my spoon. I hoped the steamy white meat under the skin would taste like chicken. It did not. I wasn't sure what it tasted like, but I wish I hadn't put it in my mouth.

A couple of nights ago, Ethan needed medical assistance. He'd gotten an insect bite on his calf that had gone septic and was very painful. He asked me to lance it to relieve the pressure. I sterilized my knife and put the tip of the blade to the sore. It burst open, just like the snake, and a white grub came wiggling out. I should not have put the white snake flesh in my mouth. I should not have thought about Ethan's grub while I was trying to choke down the bite of snake. It was launched out of my mouth by the energy bar I had swallowed earlier instead of the owl.

After I finished retching, I looked up at Lwin and Nagathan. They were both staring at me like they had never seen a human puke before.

Alessia called out from her tent.

"Hkakabo Razi! Hkakabo Razi!"

TWO

TWELVE DAYS EARLIER, I was sitting on a canopied bed in a beautiful room inside the residence of the French embassy in Rangoon, Burma—or as the military renamed it, Yangon, Myanmar.

Alessia had left me in the bedroom to "freshen up before dinner," which would take me days, not minutes, after my twenty-four-hour flight from New York, during which I hadn't slept a minute in my excitement to see Alessia again. We hadn't seen each other since Christmas. Nearly six months earlier.

I took a long shower and came out of the bathroom with a towel wrapped around my waist to find Ethan pacing back and forth in front of my window. I hadn't seen him since our ill-fated climb in the Pamir mountains of Afghanistan, where five of our teammates had been brutally murdered. Ethan had managed to save the rest of us by paragliding off a cliff and shooting the man who had abducted us.

He didn't see me as I came out of the bathroom. I watched him pace back and forth in front of the barred windows. He reminded me of a caged cat.

Alessia's mom is the French ambassador to Myanmar. Before this posting, she was the French ambassador to Afghanistan. After the disaster in the Pamirs, Ethan had been hired as Alessia's bodyguard. I was certain that protecting Alessia had given him plenty of time outdoors, because Alessia despises being trapped inside. I was also certain that this was not enough time outdoors for Ethan. The only roof he can tolerate is the nylon top of a windblown tent.

I noticed that he had a step tracker on his wrist.

"How many steps have you taken today?" I asked.

He turned around and gave me a broad grin, then walked over and gave me a bone-crunching bear hug.

He backed away from me and laughed. "You're buck-naked, man!"

"Thanks to you!" I picked up the towel from the floor and put it back around my waist. "So how many steps?"

He looked at his tracker. "Twenty-two thousand."

It wasn't noon yet.

"Do you sleepwalk?"

"Nah. But I don't sit down much. Alessia gave this wrist thing to me. She's more interested in my step count than I am. But I have to admit that it's interesting. How many steps do you take a day?"

I had no idea. I'm not into electronic gizmos. I had a smartphone, which Mom had charged before I left New York. The only reason I had carried it was to get in touch with Alessia at the Yangon airport. Now that I was anchored, there was no reason to charge it.

"I don't know how many steps I take a day. Enough to

get me where I need to go. And not too many for the last couple of days, because I've been flying."

"That's why I don't like to fly. I feel like canned meat."

I told him that I was going to get dressed. When I came out of the bathroom, Ethan had resumed his pacing and had probably put a thousand more steps on his wrist.

"So, you've heard that Alessia's mom has been recalled to France," Ethan said.

I nodded. Alessia said that her mom might be there for a month.

"Her mom wanted her to go too, but Alessia said no way. She wanted to stay because you were coming."

"I would have happily gone to France," I said. "Much shorter flight."

"But France is not Burma," Ethan said.

I looked out the window at the busy street filled with people, motorcycles, cars, and exhaust fumes. It was worse than New York City.

"I thought you were going to stay in Afghanistan and help save snow leopards," I said.

When we were in the Pamirs, we were stalked, or followed, and maybe even saved by a snow leopard. I've thought about this cat every day since I left the Pamirs, and I still can't wrap my mind around what it was doing on the mountain. All I know is that the ghost cat appeared when we needed it and may have been as responsible as Ethan for saving us.

"I did three treks in the Pamirs looking for snow leopards and didn't see a sign of one," Ethan said. "I talked to locals, hunters, and poachers. They claimed a snow leopard hadn't been spotted in the Pamirs in decades, insisting that it had been completely hunted out."

"But we saw a snow leopard," I said.

"I know. But it's like it showed up just for us. Kind of like Zopa does. Have you heard from him?"

Zopa had been our climb leader in the Pamirs. He had also been with me on Everest. Ethan was right about him. Zopa always showed up when I needed him the most.

"Zopa doesn't write letters, send emails, text, or call. He shows up in odd places face to face. But I have heard from his grandson, Sun-jo. He was in New York a couple of months ago promoting a new line of climbing gear."

"That could have been you promoting gear," Ethan said.

"Yeah. If I wanted to sell climbing gear, which I don't. And if I had summited Everest, which I didn't."

"But you could have summited Everest," Ethan said.

I let the statement, or maybe it was an accusation, hang for a few moments. Ethan was a good friend. I didn't want to lie to him, but I didn't want to diminish Sun-jo's accomplishment, or his needed fame.

"Since I didn't summit," I said, "I guess I'll never know."

Ethan looked like he wanted to push the issue further, but he gave me a grin and let it go.

I changed the subject. "Sun-jo told me that Zopa is back at his monastery being a faithful Buddhist monk. He said that after what happened in the Pamirs, Zopa swore off climbing."

"Do you believe him?"

I shrugged. "Who knows with Zopa. He's a mystery.

You've probably heard that my dad is trying to break the record for the seven summits."

"Who hasn't?" Ethan said. "He's on track for smashing the world record."

"He hasn't climbed Everest yet. But the reason I bring it up is that he asked Zopa to climb with him. Zopa passed and told my dad not to make the attempt."

"Which your dad ignored."

"Of course."

What I didn't tell him was that Josh's climbing company, Peak Experience, was nearly bankrupt. The seven summits record was a publicity stunt. If he was successful, he'd become the most famous climber on earth and get some sweet endorsement deals. Maybe enough to get his company back on its feet. In a way the stunt was my fault. Josh hadn't said anything to me, but he had been counting on me being the youngest person, at age fourteen, to summit Everest. When I passed on the opportunity, Sun-jo got the glory and the gear endorsements. Sun-jo was technically not on Josh's team. He didn't even have a climbing permit. The Chinese blamed Josh for Sun-jo's summit. They were furious with him. It's not good to have a billion people against you. Josh and his company were banned from climbing the northern, or Tibetan, side of Everest forever. Not only that, the Chinese had an arrest warrant out for him. This had really hampered his ability to travel in Asia. If he stepped into China or any of its territories, he would be arrested immediately and thrown into prison. The Chinese also had a warrant out on Zopa, but I doubted Zopa cared.

"Your dad is a little past his prime," Ethan said gently. "He has the skills, the climbing chops, but knowing what to do and being able to physically accomplish what you want to do are two different things."

"I agree. I'm worried about him."

"Are you going to catch up with him while you're on this side of the planet?"

"That's the plan, but it'll be difficult. He doesn't really have any time between summit attempts. He's on a good track right now, but bad weather, climbing conditions, and a dozen other things could ruin his time in an instant. You know that JR, Will, and Jack are filming him?"

"Yeah."

"They can't do all the climbs themselves, so they have crews stationed on different mountains in various camps. I was kind of surprised that you didn't join them." Ethan's a good climber and had been asked to join the Pamir trip as the film crew's climbing advisor and to help out with the videography.

"What happened to us in the Pamirs was rough. I suspect they didn't want to be reminded about it by having me with them. If they had asked, I think I would have turned them down. I like this gig."

I glanced out the window again at the polluted, crowded, noisy street. "I find that hard to believe. This doesn't seem like your kind of place. There are no alpine mountains here."

"That's what most people think." Ethan opened the bedroom door. Alessia was standing there holding a large manila envelope. She stepped into the room and set it on the table beneath the window. There were two words scrawled on the outside: *Hkakabo Razi.*

"What's this H . . . I can't even pronounce it."

"Maybe that's why people don't know about it," Ethan said.

"It is pronounced Kah-kah-boo Rah-zee," Alessia said.

"What is it?"

"A mountain."

"In Burma?"

"Northern Burma on the border with China," Alessia answered.

"How tall is it?"

"Well, that's the thing. No one really knows," Ethan said. "Only a couple of people have reached the summit, and they didn't have the right GPS equipment to measure the exact height. It's thought to be the highest peak in Southeast Asia. Nineteen thousand plus."

I looked at him with suspicion. "What do you have in mind?"

"Alessia and I think we should climb Hkakabo Razi and find out if it's the tallest peak in Southeast Asia," Ethan answered.

I looked at Alessia.

"It was actually my idea," she admitted. "The Pamirs were a nightmare for us. I want to replace those terrible memories with good memories. Does this make sense? We have the whole summer to do what we like. I would like to spend it climbing a mountain with you."

The Pamir climb *had* been a nightmare, the memory of which had almost made me want to never climb again.

After a couple days of debate, we agreed to give it a try, or at least to get close enough to take a look. I had some conditions, which Alessia and Ethan readily agreed to. No cameras, cell phones, computers, tablets, or drones. I wanted to do a clean climb, an old-fashioned climb, without the chance of glory. I was sick of documentation. The only electronics we would take were GPS watches and a satellite phone, which Ethan insisted upon. As Alessia's bodyguard, he had to be able to reach the embassy in case of emergency.

THREE

ALESSIA WAS SITTING UP on her sleeping pad inside her tent.

"Pic," she said, which is French for Peak.

I kneeled down next to her. "Are you okay?" I asked her.

"Yes. Of course."

She didn't look okay. Her normally olive complexion was gray. Her beautiful pale blue eyes were swollen and bloodshot. Her long black hair was tangled and greasy-looking. She was sweating, but that was usual. We were all sweating in this steam bath, except for Lwin, who never seemed to sweat.

"You must not look at me," Alessia said. "I appear too horrible."

"Tu es belle," I lied.

"I am not beautiful."

"Drink some water." I handed her a bottle.

"Is it purified?"

"Oui."

She drank the bottle almost dry.

"I'll get you another bottle."

"No. Stay with me." She squinted. "What is on your shirt front?"

I looked down. "Nagathan threw some rotted rainforest at me." At least I hoped it was rotted rainforest, and not my snake bite and energy bar.

"The elephant, he does not like you."

"No kidding. But he doesn't like Ethan either."

"He does like Lwin."

"He tolerates Lwin like we do."

"Lwin is, how do you say? Creepy?"

"That's an understatement."

"I cannot believe that I have the malaria. I took my pills with religion. You and Ethan do not have the fever?"

"No. At least I don't think so."

"Where is Ethan?"

"He went to the village we passed through yesterday to see if they have a doctor."

Alessia laughed, which was good to see. "There will be no doctor in that village."

"I know, but it gave him something to do."

"He will not be able to even speak to them," she said. "The language. They will not even come out of their homes."

"I don't think that was because of us. I think the sound of the iron bell spooked them."

"Spooked?"

"Frightened them," I clarified, then changed the subject. "You were shouting out 'Hkakabo Razi.' That's why I came in here."

"Really? I do not remember shouting anything. I have had many strange dreams. Have I shouted anything else?"

"No." Another lie, but I didn't want to upset her. "You know, we could turn back. We don't have to climb Hkakabo Razi. I didn't come to Burma to climb a mountain. I came here to see you."

Alessia smiled. "Ethan suggested the same thing last night. I will tell you the same thing I told him. I am climbing Hkakabo Razi."

Wanting to climb a mountain and actually climbing it were two different things. At this point climbing out of the tent would have been difficult for her.

Nagathan's iron bell started clanging, and he let out a trumpet as loud as a locomotive engine. I looked through the tent opening.

Ethan had returned, and he wasn't alone. He could not possibly have gotten to the village and back in this short amount of time.

"What is it?" Alessia asked, crawling up behind me.

Ethan had five people with him and several donkeys loaded with supplies. He had Lwin pinned to the ground and was holding his *panga*.

"I'll be right back."

I hurried over to Ethan and asked what was going on.

"One of the donkeys got startled when we came into camp and kicked Lwin. He pulled his *panga* and was going to kill it. Couldn't let that happen to our guests."

He let Lwin up, but kept the knife. Lwin jumped to his feet and started shouting.

Ethan grinned and ignored him. "I told you I would bring help," he said.

It looked like he had brought an army. The porters were busily unloading the donkeys. Nagathan was stretching out on his rope, trying to reach the porters and donkeys, presumably trying to murder them like Lwin had tried to do.

"You found a doctor?"

"I said I would. Come on. I'll introduce you to Dr. Freestone."

I followed him over to the fire, where Lwin and Dr. Freestone were having a shouting match—well, Lwin was shouting. Dr. Freestone was squatting near the smoking fire, poking the half-eaten snake with a stick, talking calmly in what sounded like Lwin's dialect. He was an older man, mid to upper sixties, with long gray hair and a carefully trimmed beard. He was wearing mud-spattered nylon pants, a matching shirt, and snake-proof boots that went up almost to his knees.

He poked through the ashes with his walking stick as if he were looking for something, then looked up at me.

"You must be Peak," he said with an Australian accent. "Unusual name."

"Unusual parents." This is my standard answer when someone questions my unusual name as if I don't know it is unusual.

"Tell me, Peak, did this snake have a head when it came into camp?"

I told him that Lwin had brought the snake into camp draped over his shoulder minus its head.

"You were there when he decapitated the snake?"

I shook my head.

"Pity. I don't believe that I have ever seen this species of python before, but I would need the head to confirm this."

"Are you a herpetologist?"

Instead of answering, Dr. Freestone picked up a feather out of the ashes and held it to the light.

"Lwin ate an owl before he ate the snake," I explained.

"Lwin ate an owl?" Ethan asked.

I nodded.

"Protein is protein," Dr. Freestone said. "And to answer your question, I'm an amateur herpetologist and ornithologist."

Lwin started shouting at Dr. Freestone again. Dr. Freestone stood.

"What's he saying?" Ethan asked.

"He thinks I'm trying to take over his porter business, and he's threatening to let the iron bell loose to kill us all."

Ethan stepped toward Lwin. "I'm sick of this guy."

"No need for violence," Dr. Freestone said. "At least not yet. I take it you haven't paid him."

"Half," Ethan said.

"Good. Pay him the other half and tell him to leave. I'll take you and your gear to Hkakabo Razi for free. I'm headed that direction, anyway. I think your guide might be crackers. I would not trust him. I doubt he knows the way to the mountain."

I looked at Ethan. "What do you think?"

"I say we pay him off. And thanks, Dr. Freestone, for helping us out."

"No worries," Dr. Freestone said. "And please call me Nick. After I explain the new deal to Lwin, he will leap for joy.

The worst part of your trek is yet to come. Lwin will get paid, but he doesn't have to go."

The worst is yet to come. I didn't like the sound of that. It had already been horrible. When we got off the last train stop, we rented motorcycles to continue our northern journey. Alessia had never driven a motorcycle, and I'd only driven one once. To complicate things, we each had to carry nearly one hundred pounds of gear. One by one, the motorcycles broke down. Within eighty miles, we were on foot with three hundred pounds of gear to haul. We tried to hire porters, but no matter how much we offered, no one wanted the job. We were sorting through our gear on the side of a muddy road, deciding what we could abandon, when Lwin lumbered up on Nagathan.

Nick quietly laid out the deal for Lwin. When he finished, Lwin did not leap for joy. Instead, he started shouting again.

"What now?" Ethan asked.

"He wants more money," Nick explained. "He says it's due to him because you have embarrassed him by giving him the boot in front of his countrymen."

"I'll give him the boot," Ethan said, stepping toward Lwin with clinched fists.

This time Nick didn't stop him. Lwin could see that Ethan was dead serious. He took a step back, held his hands up, gave us an orange-toothed grin, and said something.

"He says he was just joking with you," Nick said. "Now's the time for us to smile and laugh like we believe our dear friend Lwin, so he can save face."

We smiled and laughed and patted him on the back and

paid him the agreed amount of money. Ethan reluctantly gave the *panga* back to him. Within minutes, Lwin gathered his belongings, untethered Nagathan, and was gone. We could hear the clang of the iron bell long after they disappeared into the tangle.

FOUR

IT TURNED OUT THAT NICK was not a medical doctor. He was a plant doctor. A professional botanist. I doubted a plant doctor would be able to help Alessia, but I was quickly proven wrong. His expertise was in the medicinal properties of plants. He brewed a special concoction of plants into a tea, which immediately made her feel better.

"This won't cure you," he warned Alessia. "But it will speed your recovery and relieve some of the malarial symptoms. In fact, by tomorrow you'll tell me that you're all better and ready to move on, but that won't be true. I've had malaria a dozen times. It's complete camp rest for you for a minimum of three days."

"I took my antimalaria pills," Alessia said.

"Of course you did," Nick said. "And they work about eighty-five percent of the time. You could have been bitten by a mosquito with a mutated strain of malaria that your pills are ineffective against. Your immune system is different than my immune system, or Peak's, or Ethan's. We will reevaluate you in three days."

"I am holding everyone back," Alessia said.

"Hkakabo Razi has been there for millions of years. It's not going anywhere. And there is plenty for us to do right here." He looked at Ethan and me. "I told you I would lead you to the mountain for free. That wasn't exactly true. I need a couple of climbers to collect plants for me. Have you ever climbed trees?"

We both nodded, but I hadn't climbed a tree in years.

"Good!" Nick said. "My tree climbing days are long over. It's a young man's sport. You two will be my monkeys. And I suspect that you'll wish you had just paid me to take you to the mountain."

WE DID WISH WE had just paid Nick to take us to the mountain. Being his monkeys turned out to be taxing, but interesting. I knew virtually nothing about plants, nor did Ethan. Nick tried to take care of our plant ignorance by lecturing us for several hours every evening about plant biology, rainforest ecology, and the interaction between birds, reptiles, insects, and mammals. Understanding how everything was connected did not make the forest less harsh, but it did lessen my hostility toward the sweaty environment.

Tree climbing was brutal. You would think that climbing a giant tree with branches and vines would be easy for someone who climbed mountains. It isn't. Everything in the jungle stabs, slices, pokes, bites, or stings. It's nearly impossible to get a handhold without drawing blood. Ethan got bit by two snakes. Luckily, neither was venomous. I managed to put my hand into a hornet's nest. I was wearing gloves, but some of them crawled inside the gloves, attacking both hands with what felt like blowtorches. It was the worst pain I've ever experienced. Nick crushed up a bunch of plants into a salve that took the pain away within minutes. He seemed to have a natural cure for almost every emergency.

Alessia looked like a different person after Nick's third cup of antimalaria tea. She wanted to join us in our search for specimens, but Nick nixed this: "You are confined to camp until further notice. We don't want you to have a relapse while we're cutting our way through the tangle, as Peak has so aptly named the Burmese rainforest."

Nick lived in the center of Australia in Alice Springs on his family's cattle station, or ranch, but both of his parents had been born in Burma. His mother, Mya, was Burmese; his father was British. They had lived on Nick's grandfather's teak plantation in southern Burma in a house his great-grandfather had built named Hawk's Nest. They were there when the Japanese invaded Burma during World War II.

"My grandfather was put into a Japanese POW camp," Nick explained. "My father and my mother managed to get him out, but it was a close-run thing. They escaped to Australia. After the war my father decided to sell Hawk's Nest and remain in Alice Springs. But I have been coming here two or three times a year since I was a kid. My mother's family still lives here. If it weren't for the political problems here, I would have moved to Burma long ago. There is so much yet to be discovered. So much to see."

"Too much to see," I told Nick one day when we were out collecting. "I think that's been my problem with the tangle since I got here. I'm used to cold alpine environments and mountaintops where you can see for hundreds of miles, without a tree in sight. The rainforest is hot and claustrophobic. Everything is grabbing at you."

Nick slapped an insect on his neck and laughed.

"I hear you, mate. I was never much of a mountain climber, but I did summit a few mountains in my youth, so I can give you a reasonably accurate idea of how to view rainforest and alpine ecosystems. When you look at a mountain, you don't see the details. You see it in broad strokes. It isn't until you start climbing that you see the minutiae. A rainforest is too complex for a broad view. To see it you must look *into* it. From a distance, it is incomprehensible. It is a living organism with millions and millions of moving parts, most of them interrelated and dependent upon each other."

After hearing this, I started climbing trees in slow motion, pausing between each handhold, looking closely, looking *into* the tangle I was clambering over. I collected interesting plants, amphibians, and insects. I was able to avoid snakes and hornets' nests. I took the time to watch monkeys climb with admiration. I was a pathetic climber compared to them. When I got to the top of a tree, I'd swing around the trunk, then climb down as slowly as I had climbed up. It took me hours to explore a single tree. My collection bags were bursting when I got back to the ground. Most of what Ethan and I collected was of little interest to Nick, but he appreciated the effort.

"You cannot discover something new if you aren't looking."

After a couple of days, he allowed Alessia to help him in his portable laboratory cataloging the specimens we collected. A day after this, he announced that she was well enough to travel.

"We'll pack tonight and leave early tomorrow morning before it heats up," Nick said. "It will take us a week to get to Hkakabo Razi."

"A week?" Ethan said. "By my calculations, it should only take us three days."

"Correct," Nick said. "If we were walking on a cleared path, but there are no cleared paths here. During some stretches, we will have to cut our way toward the mountain with machetes. There are several rope suspension bridges to cross, provided they are still suspended, which several will not be. And don't forget the porters. They're carrying double loads, to say nothing of the fact that I am on a collecting trip. I'm not your guide. I'm here to work. We will be stopping to collect, and—"

Nick was interrupted by one of his porters running into camp, shouting. He listened to the porter for a moment, then turned to us. "Apparently, we're going to have visitors in a few minutes. A platoon of soldiers claiming they have been trying to catch us for days."

"Why?" I asked.

Nicked shrugged. "Are your papers in order? Do you have the appropriate permits?"

I looked at Ethan. I hadn't even thought about permits. All I had was a passport with a Myanmar visa stamped on it.

"We're squared away," Ethan said.

It turns out that we were not exactly squared away.

FIVE

A BEDRAGGLED GROUP of mud-splattered soldiers came marching into camp in camouflaged fatigues, carrying assault rifles. They surrounded us in complete silence.

"Uh-oh," Nick said quietly.

A full minute ticked by without a word, then an officer marched out of the jungle into the menacing circle. Unlike his men's, his fatigues were starched and immaculately clean. It looked as if he had just stepped out of a military clothing store. He inspected his men, one by one, very slowly. The men were all sweating in the afternoon heat. The officer was not sweating. After the inspection, he turned his attention to us, examining each of us closely as if he were committing our faces to memory. When he finished, he asked in perfect English, "What are you doing here?"

Nick answered. "My name is Dr. Nicholas Freestone. I'm a botanist. Why are your men pointing weapons at us?"

The crisp officer said nothing.

Alessia spoke up. "My name is Alessia Charbonneau. My mother is the French ambassador to Myanmar."

Ethan grinned. "I'm Ethan Todd. I am Alessia's security detail. I'm here to protect her."

"Protect her with what?"

Ethan didn't answer. He could protect her with his bare hands if necessary. He was a former marine sergeant who had spent a couple of years in Force Reconnaissance, then several more years as a military policeman.

"Are you carrying a weapon?" the officer asked.

"Yep," Ethan answered.

I hadn't seen a gun. It hadn't even occurred to me that he was carrying.

"You will put it on the ground in front of you," the officer said. "Slowly."

Ethan stared at the officer for a few seconds. He was obviously thinking about whether to comply. He finally reached behind his *longyi* and pulled out a small holstered pistol and set it gently on the ground. The officer nodded to one of his men. The man stepped forward, picked up the pistol, then stepped back into the circle.

The officer looked at me. "And you?"

"Peak Marcello. I'm from New York."

He scanned us again one by one, stopping when he got to Nick. "My name is Major Thakin. Why have you been running from us?"

"We haven't," Nick answered. "Why have you been looking for us?"

"I will do the questioning," Major Thakin said. "You are my prisoners."

"You have got to be kidding. I'm friends with . . ." Nick

named several generals with almost unpronounceable names. "I have known them since they were children."

"I am in command here," Major Thakin said. "Not your friends."

"I'll let them know that when I get back to Yangon," Nick said. "How do you think that's going to go for you?"

I suppose this was the point when Major Thakin was supposed to wither under Nick's name-dropping and tell him that there had been a terrible mistake. He didn't. Instead, he smiled and informed Nick that two of the generals he had mentioned were his uncles, and the third was his grandfather.

The name-dropping and genealogy were getting a little stupid and irrelevant. The immediate problem was that we were surrounded by nine sweaty guys pointing guns at us, who looked like they were about to collapse with exhaustion. If one of them succumbed, he might accidentally spray the camp with bullets and kill us.

Alessia must have been thinking the same thing, because she slowly put her arms up in the air in surrender. She didn't look afraid. In fact, she smiled at Major Thakin as she raised her arms.

The rest of us followed suit, including the porters, who had no idea what was going on because they didn't understand English.

The hands-up gesture seemed to satisfy Major Thakin. He nodded at his men. Wearily, they lowered their rifles, but kept their index fingers on the triggers.

"May we put our arms down?" Nick asked politely.

"Perhaps in a moment," Major Thakin said. "First I have some questions."

My dad would call this a "squirt of power." Josh is always encountering things like this when he deals with authorities, especially from the military guarding mountain routes and borders. *These guys don't want mountain duty. They don't have the power they would like to have, so they use every squirt of power they do have to put you in your place.*

We waited for the questions, but the major didn't seem to be in any hurry to ask them. He called the soldier who had taken Ethan's pistol over to him. The soldier stepped up smartly and presented the gun to him. Major Thakin pulled the pistol from the holster, examined it carefully, holstered it, then clipped it onto his belt.

"Where is Lwin Mahn?" he asked.

"He and his iron bell took off a few days ago," Ethan answered.

"Iron bell?"

"Nagathan," Ethan clarified.

"The elephant Nagathan is not an iron bell," Major Thakin said.

"He's killed people," I said. "He killed a girl in the forest outside an elephant camp."

"Not unless Nagathan knows how to use a slingshot," the major said, then explained.

Which is what I meant when I wrote that we weren't exactly squared away. Lwin was the murderer, not Nagathan. He had killed his estranged girlfriend with his slingshot early one morning as she was returning home after spending the night in another camp with her new boyfriend. After murdering her, he had retrieved Nagathan and made a slow getaway on elephant back. Somewhere along the way, he exchanged Nagathan's wooden bell for an iron bell. Like exchanging a license plate on a stolen car. He knew the sound of the iron bell would keep people away from him and throw the authorities off his trail.

"But he acted like an iron bell," Ethan insisted, his hands still up in the air.

"Musth," the major said.

"What is mus—"

Nick explained, his hands still up in the air. "Periodically bull elephants go through a hormonal change, where their testosterone levels spike up to sixty times above normal. It makes them very aggressive. Sometimes even homicidal. The *oozies* tie the bulls up out of the way where they can't hurt people or other elephants until the musth passes."

"Nagathan is a prime timber elephant," the major continued. "Lwin Mahn murdered the girl, then stole the elephant. We suspect he is returning to his home in the Shan state. You have aided and abetted this criminal by hiring him as your guide."

"If we'd known, we would not have hired him," I said. Actually, we would not have hired him if we'd known what he was really like, but that was beside the point.

"How much money did you pay him?"

I had no idea. I looked at Ethan.

"Five hundred," Ethan said.

"US dollars?" the major asked angrily.

Ethan nodded.

"A violation of our monetary laws. Yet another strike

36

against you. Thanks to you, we have a criminal at large carrying a fortune in foreign currency. He will be able to buy villagers' silence all the way back to the Shan state where it will be very difficult, if not impossible, to find him."

He glared at us for a few moments, then allowed us to lower our hands. "But do not move," he added. "You are to stay exactly where you are."

He grilled us for twenty more minutes. Where had Lwin gone? What direction was he headed? What did he say when we were with him? What were Lwin's intentions?

We were no help. We knew less about Lwin than we did before the major showed up.

Ethan could no longer stand "exactly" where he was. His upper body started to fidget, then he began to move his feet, sort of marching in place. Nick was looking at him too. He knew Ethan well enough by now to realize he was about to bolt.

"I'm going to use the latrine," Nick said, heading toward the tangle. "You can shoot me in the back if you like."

Major Thakin looked displeased, but he did not shoot Nick in the back. Ethan walked over and got a couple water bottles and handed them to me and Alessia. Nick reemerged from the tangle.

"My men are hungry," Major Thakin said.

"I'll be happy to have my cook make some tucker for them." Nick said something to his porters, and they began to unpack the food boxes.

The soldiers set down their rifles, unslung their packs, and started talking to the porters. There was even an occasional smile and laughter between the two groups. Ethan grabbed the camp chairs and set them around the smoky fire. The major sat down. We joined him. Apparently the major believed our story about Lwin and we were no longer his prisoners. Green tea was served. I was kind of amazed at the shift in mood. If Ethan hadn't gotten antsy, I don't think Nick would have risked taking a toilet break and we would have still been standing where we were.

Nick spent a few minutes explaining the reason behind Lwin's abrupt departure. The major said the reason he had thought we were complicit in Lwin's escape was that his trail had vanished.

"He entered a stream, and we were unable to find Nagathan's tracks again. Elephants are easy to follow. They do not just leave footprints, they leave wide paths. We eventually picked up his trail again, but the tracks were older. They led us to your camp. You obviously were not sheltering him, but we still have the monetary law violation."

This hung in the humid air for a moment.

"That's my fault," Ethan said. "It wasn't planned. I didn't have enough kyats to pay Lwin, so I offered him US currency. I realize now that I shouldn't have, but we were desperate. Is there a way I can pay a fine directly to you to pass on to the appropriate authority?"

It was obvious to me, and probably to everyone else, that Ethan was attempting to bribe the major. By the way he was handling it, this was not the first time he had bribed an official.

Major Thakin appeared to think for a second or two, then said, "Yes, I think that can be arranged."

"How many kyats do you think it would cost?"

"Probably more than you are carrying. Do you still have US dollars?"

"Some."

"Three hundred dollars?"

Ethan shook his head. "Not quite."

This wasn't true. He had over a thousand dollars hidden in his money belt, half of which was mine. I'd asked him to stow it for me because I hadn't thought to bring a money belt with me.

"If it is close to that amount, I think that will cover the violation. I will have to exchange the dollars for kyats, but that will not be an inconvenience, as one of my cousins is a banker."

"I really appreciate you taking care of this for me."

"Think nothing of it."

"The money is in my tent. I'll get it."

The money was tied beneath his *longyi,* but he couldn't very well pull the wad out in front of the major, or the men, although they were happily chowing down with the porters at the edge of camp and paying no attention to us. Ethan returned with a roll of money hidden in his fist. He slipped it to the major like a magician making a card disappear. The major glanced over at his men, then slipped it into his tunic pocket with the same sleight of hand that Ethan had used to give it to him, and our legal problems were over, or so we thought.

"I suppose I should look at your passports, visas, and permits while I'm here," the major said pleasantly. "May I have another cup of tea? And it smells like the rice is done."

Our papers were in Alessia's tent. We gave the major the stack of documents. He looked them over carefully as he sipped his tea and ate his rice. When he finished, he set them to the side and examined Nick's papers.

"Dr. Freestone," he said, "your papers are in perfect order, but I'm afraid there are some issues with your friends' papers."

Here we go again, I thought.

"Your permit says that you have permission to explore the area *around* Hkakabo Razi. There is no mention of climbing the mountain, and yet you have a lot of climbing equipment." He pointed to the climbing gear stacked outside our three tents, which we'd been about to sort through and pack when he and his men marched into camp.

How much is this going to cost us? I thought.

"You never know what you're going to run into getting over to Hkakabo Razi," Nick said. "As you know, there are several suspension bridges on the way. Every time I've been there, one or two of them have been down and had to be restrung. The climbing equipment they brought is not for mountain climbing. We are using it to climb trees. These young people volunteered to help me collect specimens."

"Are you saying that your meeting out here was pre-arranged?" the major asked incredulously.

"Yes."

I wondered if there was a national law against telling big fat whoppers.

"Ethan and I met at a party at the French embassy. He said he and some friends were coming out this way to do some trekking the same time I was going to be here. We didn't have a firm date, or even a specific place to meet, but I told him that if he and his friends wanted to lend a hand, I would be very grateful. I told him to bring climbing gear. We never seem to have enough rope."

I hoped Nick hadn't just given the major enough rope to hang us. Major Thakin was clearly skeptical of Nick's explanation, but there was no way to prove or disprove it out here in the tangle, or even back in Yangon, for that matter. Nick was well connected, and even though Major Thakin had blown off Nick's generals earlier, I think he'd had time to reconsider. And we had all seen him pocket the bribe, which I'm sure he didn't want his commanding officers to know about.

"We will spend the night here," Major Thakin said.

SIX

I'm lying in my tent shrouded by mosquito netting, waiting for dawn with my headlamp lighting this sweat-proof journal. Outside, the snoring soldiers nearly drown out the sounds of the jungle. We will get a late start this morning. The porters will have to make breakfast for the soldiers, then we will have to pack, which means we'll start cutting our way toward the mountain during the heat of the day. This doesn't matter to me. I just want to get moving. I'm suffocating here. It's like I'm underwater trying to reach the surface where I can breathe. I dream of the alpine slopes of Hkakabo Razi . . .

"ARE YOU AWAKE, PEAK? I saw your light. I didn't mean to —"

Alessia had put her head through the flap of my tent. "No, no, come on in. I nodded off, but I'm awake now."

"Nodded?" Alessia doesn't always understand American jargon.

"Dozed off. Fell asleep, briefly."

"Oh." She crawled in the rest of the way.

There wasn't much headroom in our two-person alpine tents, so she lay down next to me beneath my mosquito netting, which was nice. This was the first time we'd been alone together in almost a week, except for when I was tending her during her fever, which didn't count because she wasn't exactly herself.

"You were writing in the journal," she said quietly so as not to disturb the sleeping soldiers.

"Yes. But I only started it a few days ago."

"Will you read some to me?"

I didn't like reading aloud. And I didn't like anyone reading my stuff until I'd had a chance to revise it. I'd already written things that I knew no one was ever going to see. My hesitation answered Alessia's question.

"You do not have to read it to me," she said.

"I'd rather not at this point. I'll let you read it after I've fixed it."

"Like the journal you kept about us in the Pamirs," she said.

"Right."

Alessia smiled. "I can wait. Do you believe that Lwin is a murderer and a thief?"

"His girlfriend getting killed by a slingshot doesn't look good. Stealing a timber elephant and running doesn't look good either. I'd say he's probably guilty."

"I think the major will not stop until he apprehends him."

I agreed. Major Thakin didn't appear to be the kind of man who gave up on anything he began. Light started shining through the red tent fabric. We switched off our headlamps and watched the red brighten. Our peaceful sunrise was interrupted by an elephant trumpeting loud enough to shake the tent. I grabbed my ice ax and tumbled out of the tent, thinking that Nagathan had returned to crush us.

He hadn't. He was standing at the edge of our camp surrounded by three *oozie*s, one on his right, one on his left, and one sitting on his neck. Lwin was not among them. Nagathan's trunk was raised to his forehead in what looked like a salute. He was no longer trumpeting.

The camp was in complete chaos with soldiers running around buttoning their tunics, grabbing their rifles. The porters were scampering up the tree trunks like monkeys. Nick was standing outside his tent watching the disorder with an amused expression. Ethan crawled out of his tent scratching his wild hair, blinking himself awake.

He looked over at Alessia and me. "Why are you carrying an ice ax?"

I nodded at Nagathan.

"Whoa! He's back!" Ethan stared at the bull elephant for a moment, then asked, "You notice anything different about him?"

"He's standing at attention, and he's not throwing jungle ooze at me."

"He is wearing a wooden bell," Alessia said.

She was right. The iron bell had been replaced by a wooden bell. I took a closer look to make sure it was Nagathan and not some other timber elephant. There was a tear on the bottom of his left ear. His right tusk was shorter than his left, and there was a chip of ivory missing on the end. It was definitely Nagathan, but the wooden bell wasn't the only difference. There was something about his behavior.

"He's calm," I said. "His eyes aren't wild. He's not rocking back and forth."

"He's surrounded by three *oozie*s with elephant hooks," Ethan pointed out.

"Yeah, but they aren't using the hooks on him. They are as relaxed as he is. They look like they're ready to go out into the forest and harvest teak."

Nick walked over to us. "What a difference a few days makes," he said. "Looks like Nagathan has finished his musth and is back to his sane self. Did you notice the blood on his right tusk?"

We were too far away to see in any detail, but it did look like there was a smear of red on the tusk. Nagathan lowered his trunk.

"That's not good," Nick said.

"What?" Ethan asked.

"The darkish area on his forehead and down the front of his trunk. I think it's blood as well. Something bad has happened in the forest."

Major Thakin shouted out several orders. His soldiers buttoned their shirts, formed a straight line, shouldered their guns, and stood at attention. It looked like there were twice as many soldiers as there had been the day before. Nagathan and the *oozie*s had not arrived in camp alone. The soldiers from the previous day were not the only patrol Major Thakin had with him. He had probably spent the night in order to rest half his men.

He paced up and down the line, questioning the new arrivals one by one, then he walked over and started talking to the *oozie*s.

We looked at Nick.

"It appears that our old friend Lwin is dead. They found him late last night. Nagathan pounded him into a pulp. According to the soldiers, he was unrecognizable as a human. The forest animals had been feeding on what was left of him for a couple of days. It was too dark to search for remains last night, so the soldiers camped near the crime scene. This morning they searched the area and found a foot, two fingers, and a bloody *longyi* up in a tree. Nagathan may have thrown it up into the branches after pulverizing him. The three *oozie*s have been with the major since the pursuit began. They are from a different elephant camp than Lwin. I wondered how the soldiers were going to get Nagathan back where he belonged. He must have picked them up along the way. Drafted, so to speak. I'm sure they will be happy to get back to their camp and families."

"So, Nagathan's musth has passed?" I said.

"It appears so, but not soon enough for Lwin. Elephants in musth are very dangerous. It speaks well for Lwin's skill to have gotten him this far without getting someone killed. The patrol found Nagathan tied up between two trees. He had eaten every leaf and branch within reach. If they hadn't found him, he would have starved."

"What about the iron bell?" Alessia asked.

"According to the soldiers, the *oozie*s carved a wooden bell last night and put it on him this morning. They say he's been a perfect gentleman since they untied him."

Major Thakin came back with a bloody *longyi* and dropped it at our feet. Wrapped inside were the foot and two fingers.

Alessia looked away from the mess. I wanted to look away too, but I couldn't.

"Is this him?" The major asked.

I didn't know about the foot and the fingers, but the bloody *longyi* was definitely Lwin's. Red with bright yellow squiggles. He had three *longyi*s the exact same color and pattern. He offered to sell one to me when Ethan and Alessia started wearing the skirts.

"It must be," Ethan said.

Major Thakin nodded to one of his men. The soldier picked up the parts and hauled them away.

"What will you do with the remains?" Alessia asked.

"Take them back to headquarters."

I didn't know how far headquarters was, but I doubted the foot and the fingers would be recognizable by the time they got there. One thing the tangle did not have was ice. I hadn't seen a cube since we left Yangon.

"Perhaps you should take the *longyi* and leave the . . ." Alessia hesitated. "The parts here. We could take photographs. You could use the photograph to prove—"

"Yes, yes," the major interrupted. "A good idea. You get the photographs and perhaps a plastic bag for the *longyi*, while I get my men organized. I want to start before the day heats up."

So did we.

Ethan and I took the gruesome photos with the major's

digital camera, while Alessia packed our gear. Before the major gave us complete possession of the fingers, he took a close-up of the print in the morning light.

PART

TWO

Bridges

SEVEN

I'm leaning against a tree trunk as wide as my bedroom wall at home. We are camped at the entrance to a suspension bridge. Our first. Four donkeys. Eight people. I think the donkeys are calmer about the crossing than we are. Or maybe they are just happy to have been relieved of their burdens. The donkeys can't cross the narrow bridge loaded down with our gear. We're going to have to haul stuff across the bridge ourselves. It will take several trips back and forth, and we cannot possibly finish before dark.

We've taken our time through the tangle the past two days, stopping here and there to climb trees and collect samples for Nick. It turns out that Alessia is a better monkey than Ethan and me. She climbs faster, manages to come back to ground with fewer bites, stings, and scrapes, and Nick gets very excited with her finds.

Right now Alessia and Ethan are climbing down to the river-bed—a sheer green wall covered with vines, branches, and plants—about a thousand feet below the bridge. I decided not to go, telling them that I thought at least one of us should stay alive to get to the top of Hkakabo Razi. I was joking of course. The reason I stayed behind is to chill for a couple of hours, if chill is the right word in the heat of the jungle, which hasn't been too bad the past two days. Or maybe I'm acclimatizing to it, and to the closeness of the rainforest. I've actually been enjoying myself, although I'm still pining for the alpine. A glass of glacial ice water would be nice right now.

Nick has set up a makeshift awning and is examining and cataloging our latest finds, using a magnifying glass and portable microscope with a mirror beneath the slide tray to catch the light. After he's examined the plant or flower, he takes a photograph of it.

Three of the porters are sleeping near a smoky fire. The fourth is with the donkeys. They hobble them in the late afternoon and set them free for a few hours to poke around for food. The porters take turns guarding the donkeys from tigers. There aren't many tigers in Burma anymore, because poachers kill them and sell their parts to the Chinese for more money than illegal drugs. I'm not sure what the porters, only armed with *panga*s, could do against a tiger anyway.

The tree I'm leaning against is next to the bridge on the edge of the ravine. If I lean forward, I can see Alessia and Ethan clambering down the wall. I'm betting that when they get to the bottom, they are going to cross the river, climb up the other side, and walk across the bridge to camp. That's what I would do.

The bridge is four hundred feet long. According to Nick, it's the shortest we are going to cross. "And the best of the bunch," he told us. "We'll be crossing several more before we reach Hkakabo Razi. One or two of them will be out. If we can't repair them, we'll have to go around. With the pack animals, that could take some time. More time than you probably want to spend getting to the mountain. You may want to push on in a more direct manner."

"We'll cross that bridge when we come to it," Ethan said.

Nick and I laughed, then had to explain the play on words to Alessia.

The bridge is made of rope woven from tree bark. It's shaped like a V. On the bottom of the V are slippery rough-hewn planks a little over two feet wide. On the top of the V is a rope rail. There isn't a hunk of metal on it. The rope anchors are wrapped around the trunks of ancient trees. The entire bridge is made out of re-purposed forest.

Alessia and Ethan have made it down to the riverbed and are attempting to cross. Alessia is in the lead. I pull my binoculars out. She finds a tree that has fallen to the opposite bank. She's halfway across before Ethan sees she's found a route. She moves lithely, with perfect balance, over the slippery trunk as if she were on a paved path, reaching the other side thirty yards ahead of Ethan. He slips as he jumps off the tree and gets soaked in the shallows. Alessia laughs and points up to the wall of green in front of them. They study the wall for several minutes, then start their ascents, each using a different route. It's a race. I would have picked a different route from either of theirs, but I have the advantage of seeing the entire wall. Alessia is moving quickly and smoothly, but Ethan has picked a better way to the top. He beats her by a minute.

"I'LL GO FIRST," NICK SAID early the next morning. He was loaded down with enough gear to crush a donkey.

"Maybe we should lighten your load," I suggested. "You don't have to haul all of the gear in one load."

He smiled. "Nonsense. It just looks bulky. Most of it is dried plants. I think we should go one at a time. Who's next?"

"I'll go," I said.

"Good. We'll take the animals last."

We watched him cross.

"The boards are very slippery," Alessia said. "The bridge, it wiggles. And the ropes give splinters in your hands. Do you have gloves?"

"Yeah, we all do," Ethan said. "Peak brought his cold weather gear for when he catches up with his dad."

"Mittens won't work on those ropes," I said. "But ridiculously, I do have a pair of light climbing gloves." I pulled them out. Mom had stuffed them into my pack just before I left the apartment. Gloves are not something you need in sweltering Yangon, and she didn't know I was going to try for Hkakabo Razi, or be crossing rope bridges. They were half-finger climbing gloves, which I never use. I prefer to climb with just chalk on my hands, because gloves make your hands sweat. I put them on and started across.

It didn't just wiggle, as Alessia put it — the bridge swayed wildly and vibrated with every step I took. It was like walking a loose tightrope. But she was right about the boards being slippery. The long span across the ravine was shaped like a U. It was worse going down with my pack pushing me forward than it was going up with the pack dragging me back. But with all that, I still made pretty good time, as did everyone else, getting everything across except for the donkeys.

One porter stayed with the donkeys each trip with our supplies. When we had everything across, a second porter joined the lone porter to help lead the donkeys.

"We have to bring them over together," Nick explained. "They won't go alone—herd instinct—but they'll do fine roped together. Strength in numbers and all that."

The string started across, single file, tied together, a porter in the lead, a porter in the rear.

All went well until they were about fifty feet away from us. The lead donkey suddenly jumped and kicked the donkey behind, which caused a chain reaction. The donkeys lost their footing and started sliding backward on the slick planks. Their legs tangled. The bridge started swaying wildly. Ethan and I shot forward to help, but Nick stopped us.

"No! Let it settle!"

It was hard to do nothing with the porters clinging to the rope railings for dear life and the donkeys braying in terror.

"The anchors, they look good!" Alessia shouted from behind us.

She'd had the sense to check the only things stopping the bridge from plunging into the raging river. It took several minutes for the bridge to settle down and a couple more minutes for the first porter to stir. He slowly untangled his legs from the lead donkey and got to his feet. He said something to the other porter, who then also stood. The donkeys remained where they were, two of them on their knees, two on their sides. They were either too frightened to stand or knew to wait for the porters to get them up. The porters gently coaxed them, one by one, to a standing position. When they were all up, the string finished the crossing as if nothing terrible had happened, except for the two porters loading quids of betel nut into their mouths with trembling hands to calm their nerves.

Nick talked to them for a few moments about what had happened.

"They say that the lead donkey was stung or bitten," he translated. "The best thing to get past this is to move."

An hour later, we were back on the narrow trail. We didn't stop to climb a tree or collect a single plant. Nick wanted to get over the second bridge before dark.

"There's a village a few kilometers on the other side," he said. "Or there was a couple of seasons ago when I was last here. They have a market. I'm getting low on essentials. Rice, tea, sugar, flour. If I don't replenish soon, I might have to make myself a slingshot."

We were getting a little low on food too, because we were trying to keep most of it in reserve for Hkakabo Razi, where there wouldn't be any food. A slingshot wouldn't help us. There was nothing to shoot above fifteen thousand feet.

The second bridge was shorter, more substantial, and twice as wide as the first bridge. Nick didn't bother unpacking the donkeys, which saved us a couple hours. They trotted across so fast they nearly trampled the lead porter.

We reached the outskirts of the village at dusk, tired, sweaty, and filthy, but happy to have made such good time. A girl and a boy, maybe eight or nine years old, ran up to us smiling. The girl held her hand out and opened it. Lying on her palm was a tiny monkey foot.

"Good lord," Nick said.

EIGHT

THE VILLAGE WAS NOT A VILLAGE. It was a bustling town ten times bigger than when Nick had last seen it. There were hundreds of people selling everything from tiger eyes to roasted dogs. Alessia and I split off from Ethan and Nick to wander around the market on our own. Half the people buying and selling were Chinese wearing western-style clothes, carrying duffel bags of cash slung over their shoulders like supersized purses. They were buying animal parts, skins, rubies, and opium. They were selling, or trading, knockoff luxury watches, bags, western apparel, and electronics, which couldn't be charged because there was no power.

"Boomtown," I said.

"Boom? An explosion?"

"In a way." I told her about the boomtowns that had popped up in the American West near gold and silver mines in the 1800s.

"A different kind of gold and silver," Alessia said. "The vein will run dry when they kill all of the animals in the forest."

I wondered how they had gotten all of this stuff to market without roads. This was answered when we reached the far end of town. A large clearing had been carved out of the forest. In it were donkeys, elephants, oxen, and empty carts. Nick's porters had made camp next to the makeshift corral. I hoped we weren't staying there. The smell was making my eyes water. We waved at the porters, but they didn't notice us. They were too busy talking to the other porters. I suspected that in the short amount of time they had been there, they'd learned more about this place than we would ever know.

"We are strangers in a strange land," Alessia said.

"You're right about that."

"I think we should call it Strangeland."

"Perfect." I took her hand. "I guess we better try to find Ethan and Nick and see—"

A small helicopter flew in low over the trees and began to descend into the corral. Elephants trumpeted, and donkeys brayed. The porters glanced up, then went back to their conversation as if a helicopter coming in for a landing in the middle of nowhere was as common as rain in the rainforest. We waited to see who got out. I figured it was a military helicopter, but it wasn't. The men climbing out of the doors were civilians. Two armed men emerged first, followed by another man with a big duffel bag over his shoulder. The last man to step off was wearing white slacks, a white shirt, and a white Panama hat. He said something to the man with the duffel, who started toward town. The guy in white and the other two men watched him for a moment, then turned and started walking toward the trees. All four men were Asian.

"Who do you think that is?" Alessia asked.

"Whoever it is makes enough money to travel by helicopter, which is a lot easier than how we got here." I pointed at the pack animals in the corral. "And everyone else."

"But they only see the tops of the trees. It is the difference between seeing a mountain from afar and climbing it. No?"

"Yes. You've been spending too much time with Nick."

"He is very smart."

"Yes he is."

I kissed her.

WE DIDN'T FIND ETHAN until after dark. Actually, we didn't find him—Ethan found us. We were wandering through the lantern-lit market, going from stall to stall, asking in halting Burmese where our friend was. We walked into a shop that sold tea and smoked dog, among other things, and found Ethan trying to ask the proprietor where we were. We left with a tin of tea, but passed on the dog meat.

An old friend of Nick's, Thuta Soe, had invited us to spend the night at his house. Thuta's house was outside of the town, or Strangeland, along a small river. Like most Burmese homes, the house was built on stilts to protect it from flooding during the monsoon and prevent venomous snakes from getting inside. Most of the houses we'd seen in the forest had one, or maybe two, single-level rooms. They were built almost entirely out of bamboo—easily repaired or replaced if they were blown or washed away. Thuta's house was five times bigger than any of the houses I'd seen in the tangle. It was three stories high and lit up like a skyscraper at night.

"Something, isn't it?" Ethan said. "Thuta's had to re-build three times. Two fires. One typhoon. He says his house gets better every time. Wait until you see the inside."

We followed him up the ladder-like steps to the veranda. Someone was cooking something that made my mouth water. We took off our muddy shoes before stepping inside. The floor was made out of woven bamboo and covered with bamboo mats like all the other stilted houses I'd been in. It was like walking on a firm mattress. The first time I had walked on a bamboo floor, I thought I was going to fall through and land where the pigs were wallowing beneath the house. I was trying to keep my feet on the joists when the man who had invited me inside saw what I was doing and started jumping up and down on the spongy floor to demonstrate that it was safe.

A woman wearing a colorful *longyi* came through an open doorway to our left and gave us a bright smile.

"Men upstairs," she said.

I returned the smile and looked past her into the other room, where the delicious smell was coming from. Savory smoke was rising from a large wok heated by a charcoal flame.

"It smells wonderful," Alessia said,

"Yes. Yes. But not for you. For children. You come with me. I show. You two boys go upstairs. Old men there."

I would have rather gone into the kitchen to see, and hopefully taste, what was sizzling in that wok, but I obeyed and followed Ethan up the stairs.

Nick and Thuta were sitting on the floor next to a blanket covered with dried plants and flowers. A bright lantern hung above the blanket. They were both holding magnifying glasses. Thuta got to his feet, put his palms together, and bowed.

"Are you a botanist too?" I asked.

"Hardly," Thuta answered in English. "I am merely an interested amateur."

"A very gifted amateur," Nick said. "Thuta has found some astonishing specimens, two of which I have never seen before."

Thuta beamed with pleasure at the compliment. Ethan offered him the tin box of tea we had bought at the shop in the market.

"That is very kind of you. Dr. Freestone and I have been friends since I was a boy, and before that, he was a friend of my father's. My home is his home and, in turn, your home. Gifts are unnecessary. I hope you did not pay too much for this."

We bought the tea because Alessia liked the box. I didn't know we were going to give it to him. I don't think Ethan knew it either. He's impulsive. He gave the box to Thuta because the box was in his hands. Simple as that.

"You met my wife, Yati, downstairs?" Thuta asked. "The beautiful woman cooking?"

"Alessia is in the kitchen with her," Ethan answered.

I could still smell the aroma wafting through the porous bamboo floors. My stomach grumbled.

"Ah, yes, dinner. Yati was preparing a Burmese feast for you, but at the last minute, you received another dinner invitation. Do not worry. The food will not go to waste. We will share it with the poorer children. Your loss will be their gain. They will be grateful."

We had seen a lot of kids in the market begging, who looked like they could use a good meal. Alessia and I had given two of them some change and watched them happily run over to the betel nut vendor, buy a couple of quids, and pop them into their little mouths. After this we stopped giving out spare change.

"Does this village have an official name?" I asked Thuta.

He laughed. "The official answer is no, it does not. My grandfather was a trader. He brought our family here and built a home because of its close proximity to China, India, and Tibet before it came under Chinese rule. Soon other family members and friends moved here, then porters and their families. It became more of a trading post than a village."

"It looks more like a town now," Ethan said.

"That is a recent development. An unfortunate situation really, which I have no control over. Eventually the town will become unprofitable and everyone will move away, but I will remain, along with my family and friends, eking out our living in the jungle as we always have."

Thuta spoke with a slight British accent. "Your English is very good," I said.

"Thank you. That is because of Dr. Freestone. One of his graduate students lived with us for nearly three years. In exchange for room and board, he taught our family English and other subjects. With his help, I was able to matriculate and go to the university."

"But you came back here."

"There was never any doubt about that. This is my home, or it will be again when everyone leaves."

It didn't appear to me that anyone was leaving anytime soon.

"I didn't see any soldiers in town," Ethan said.

"That is because we do not exist." Thuta smiled at me. "Officially. But the military does come here every few weeks to collect unofficial taxes so that we may remain nonexistent. They have spies here so they know what they are due. I think you call this ransom in your country."

"Extortion," Ethan corrected.

"Ah yes, that is the word. My father paid extortion too. It is the way of the jungle. But enough of this. You do not want to be late for dinner."

"Where are we going to dinner?" Nick asked.

"A wealthy businessman invited you. He's a relative newcomer to the village. You will like him. He is interested in westerners. It is not unusual for him to invite people to dinner in order to know them better."

"How did he find out about us?" Alessia asked.

Thuta smiled. "This is a small place. Everyone knows everything about everybody."

NINE

THE FULL MOON FILTERED through the giant trees lighting the narrow path along the river. We walked past several more stilted houses, but none as elaborate as Thuta's. He said that most of the houses along the river belonged to his children and relatives.

"That is my daughter's home," he said, pointing. "Over there is my son's home. It is small because he is not yet married."

"Can anyone build along the river?" Ethan asked.

"Certainly. We do not own the river. But few people build out here. They prefer to live in town. My family has always lived out here. My grandfather was fond of saying, 'What is the point of living in the forest if you do not live in the forest?'"

The houses became fewer in between until there were none left. All that remained was the moon, the trail, and the river. I was about to ask Thuta how much farther it would be when we rounded a corner and saw our destination. It was a house, a very big house, built on a promontory overlooking the river. It was two stories, built out of hardwood. It was not on stilts. A tall, sturdy fence surrounded it, lit with powerful electric floodlights.

"Generator," Ethan said.

"Yes," Thuta said. "A small one for the security lights."

"What's the man's name?" Nick asked, sounding a little irritated.

"I didn't tell you? I am so sorry. You are having dinner with Mr. Chin. He built this house two years ago."

"What kind of business is he in?" Ethan asked.

Thuta didn't answer, because a wooden gate opened in front of us.

Ethan pointed to the top of the fence and whispered, "Surveillance cameras and motion detectors. High-end gear. Armed men on rooftop. Ten o'clock and two o'clock. I'll take the lead."

I glanced up. Two shadowy figures. It was too dark to see if they were armed or not, but I believed him. Ethan had a trained eye for that kind of thing.

"More spots on the roof," Ethan mumbled. "Manually operated. That way they can blind intruders."

Ethan was in full bodyguard now, standing directly in front of Alessia to shield her from any kind of threat. An elaborately carved front door swung open, and a man stepped out. He gave us a small bow.

"Welcome to my home. My name is Zhang Wei, but please call me Chin as all my friends do. Please come inside."

It was the man in the Panama hat from the helicopter, minus the hat. His white linen suit stood out in the dim light of the inner fence. We followed him into a large lantern-lit room that smelled of kerosene, incense, and fried food. The food cooking did not smell as good as Yati's, but it was close. In front of us was a screened veranda overlooking the river. The hardwood floor had no bounce to it. On our right was a long dining table set with plates, utensils, cloth napkins, and glasses. At the head of the table was a set of stairs leading up to the second floor. On our left was a door that led to what must have been the kitchen because that was where the good smells were coming from. All in all, the layout was like Thuta's, but enlarged and solid. The big room was rustically furnished with carved teak benches and chairs. We had been in a shop that day with handmade furniture very much like this.

"Can you find your way back?" Thuta asked.

"You are not dining with us?" Chin inquired.

"I cannot. I must return and help Yati."

"Pity," Chin said.

"We can find our way back," Nick said, looking a little confused.

I was confused too. Thuta bowed and walked back outside. I didn't think that Yati needed his help. Maybe he preferred her food to Chin's. I nearly followed him.

"I guess introductions are in order." Chin looked at Nick. "You must be Dr. Freestone. I know of you, but I have not read your papers. My passion is for gems, not plants, but I have heard nothing but praise for your work." He turned to me.

"Peak Marcello," I said.

"Good to meet you . . . Peak? As in summit?"

I nodded.

"For some reason, you look familiar. Is that possible?"

"I don't see how. This is my first time in Burma."

Chin shrugged and looked at Ethan, who gave him a grin.

"Ethan Todd."

"I don't know that name, but you too look familiar.

"Just one of those faces," Ethan said. "Thanks for inviting us to dinner."

"Think nothing of it. You are doing me a favor. It sometimes gets lonely out here."

That was hard to believe with two men posted on the roof, probably another upstairs. His security guys hadn't looked very domestic, which meant there was at least one more person in the kitchen cooking.

Chin turned his attention to Alessia and looked surprised.

"You are Alessia Charbonneau, are you not?"

Now Alessia looked surprised. "We know each other?"

"No, we have never met, but I saw you at the French embassy in Yangon during a reception for your mother. There were many . . ." He looked back at Ethan. "You were there too! I remember now. You were watching everyone, looking uncomfortable in a suit and tie."

Ethan laughed. "That was probably me, all right."

It was hard to imagine Ethan in a suit and tie. It was hard to imagine that he owned a suit and tie. He was wearing lightweight nylon pants and a T-shirt. So was Alessia. They had both changed into western clothes at Thuta's.

"Security?" Chin asked.

Ethan nodded. "The only downside to the job is the suit. Luckily, I don't have to wear it very often."

Chin stepped back and looked at us, smiling. I noticed

he was missing the index finger and thumb on his left hand. "I have put it all together," he said enthusiastically. "Later I will tell you what I have discovered. Come out onto the veranda for refreshments."

I wasn't sure what he meant by his discovery, but what I discovered on the veranda was lemonade with ICE. I downed it without taking the glass away from my lips. Alessia laughed, but I noticed that she had gulped down most of her glass too. Nick and Ethan had passed on the lemonade and were drinking cold beers.

Alessia and I took our freshly filled glasses to the end of the veranda away from everyone. Chin had cut down a few of the trees along the river. We leaned over the rail and, in the moonlight, could see the water clearly thirty feet below.

"What do you think of Chin?" Alessia asked quietly.

"I'm not sure, but I'm happy for the ice."

"Soon we will have all the ice we want. Glacial ice."

"I'm looking forward to it. How are you feeling?"

"I am fine—well, perhaps a little weak still."

"Maybe we should rest here another day." I took several gulps of lemonade.

"Ha. You just want to drink more cold lemonade. I want to go to the mountain. I do not know how well this man knows my mother. He may contact her, or the embassy, and tell them where we are. Mother believes we are trekking in the forest."

"You didn't tell her about Hkakabo Razi?"

Alessia shook her head. "Did you tell your mother?"

"Yes." The deal I have with Mom is that I don't have to ask permission, but I have to tell her what I'm up to. If I don't and get hurt, or die, she will dig me up and kill me again. She wasn't thrilled about the climb, but she was happy I had told her. "Maybe you should tell her," I said.

"She is very busy," Alessia said. "I don't want to worry her."

Which, I interpreted as *I don't want to get in an argument with her.* I shrugged. It wasn't my place to tell Alessia what to do. "Chin can't get in touch with her from here," I said.

"He has a satellite phone on a table next to the front door. You did not see it?"

I shook my head. Our sat phone had gone dead. We hadn't discovered this until we tried to use it when Alessia's malaria had worsened. Ethan had forgotten to turn it off when we were looking for alternative transportation after the motorcycles came unhinged.

"As far as Chin knows, we are trekking in the forest. I doubt Ethan or Nick will tell him about our plans for Hkakabo Razi."

"But if he tells my mother where we are, she will know our intentions. I am not terribly concerned about what will happen to me if my mother finds out about the mountain, but I am concerned about Ethan. She might dismiss him."

"I'm sure he's thought about that. I don't want to sound harsh, but I doubt he cares about being fired." Alessia looked hurt. "Don't get me wrong, he likes you a lot. I'm sure he likes your mom too. But this is the longest time he's held the same job since he was in the marines. He's an adrenaline junkie, and I doubt he's getting what he needs dressed in a suit and tie at an embassy function."

I had to rephrase this so she would understand what I was saying. When I finished, she smiled.

"I think I too am this adrenaline junkie," she said. "Perhaps it is so with you."

"I'm not sure what I am, but I do love to climb."

An older Burmese woman came out onto the veranda and said, "Food ready now."

The food was incredibly good. As we wolfed it down with glass after glass of ice water, Chin explained that he had four houses like this along Burma's borders, staffed by trusted older couples. The woman from the veranda cooked and cleaned. Her husband did maintenance in and around the house. He didn't mention the men from the helicopter. His main residence was in Yangon, not far from the French embassy. He made a circuit of his border homes every two or three weeks to buy, trade, or sell. He was vague about what he was buying, trading, and selling, but he made it sound like his main source of income was selling gems. I thought it was more likely that he was in the drug trade. How else could he afford the helicopter, homes, and security guys?

He and Nick got into a long conversation about rare Burmese orchids, which Chin believed could be exported and sold for duffel bags of cash. Nick insisted that orchids and other rainforest flowers should be left in situ, or in place, because not enough was known about the symbiotic relationships of plant species. Chin asked Nick what the difference was between Nick picking a plant and taking it to Australia to examine, and someone else taking a plant to another country to germinate it.

"Science," Nick answered.

"Why not have science pay for itself?" Chin asked. "I am

sure, at times, you struggle for grants to fund your research and collecting expeditions."

Nick admitted that funding was difficult, but he insisted that the only way to practice pure science was to keep it separate from commercial profit.

Chin smiled and held his hands up in defeat. "You win, Dr. Freestone. At least this round, but I reserve the right to revisit the subject again with you in the future." He reached into his jacket and pulled out a gold business card case with a large dark ruby set into it. "This is the first pigeon blood ruby I purchased many years ago. I sold it at a good price, tripling my investment. This money allowed me to buy other gems. After a time, I began to wonder what had happened to this ruby. I began looking for it. It took me years to find it again. The owner charged me a hundred times more for the gem than I had paid for it, but it was a bargain. I would have paid a thousand times more for this ruby."

I guessed that this was the discovery he had been talking about.

He passed the case to Nick. "Please take a card. If you need anything, just write or call me. The number is my satellite phone. Pass the case on. I want all of you to have my contact information."

Nick passed the case to me. The ruby looked almost black in the lantern light. It was beautiful. I handed the case to Alessia, and she passed it on to Ethan.

"That's a big stone," Ethan said. "How many karats is it?"

"Almost eight."

Ethan looked at the card. "What kind of sat phone do you use?"

"An Iridium 9575. Why do you ask?"

"We have the same model, but our battery is dead."

"I will give you a fully charged battery. I have several spares. You are continuing north tomorrow?"

"First light," Nick answered.

Chin looked at the ruby one more time before slipping the case back into his suit jacket. "And now for my discovery," he said with relish. "Or I should say, discoveries." He looked at me. "Peak, your father is Joshua Wood, the famous mountain climber. He is attempting to break the seven summits record. Ethan, you snowboarded down Mount McKinley chased by a pack of wolves. Alessia, you participated in the Peace Climb in the Pamir mountains of Afghanistan with these two, and there are rumors that you had a bad climb."

We had managed to keep our Pamir problem relatively quiet so as to not overshadow the purpose of the Peace Climb. Those of us who survived swore to say nothing more than that some of the climbers had died, when in fact, they were murdered.

"Right on all counts," Ethan said. "Do you follow climbing?"

"In my youth I was a climber," Chin said. "I was a member of the Chinese climbing team. But that was a long time ago. Two of my nephews are now on the Chinese team."

Which probably meant that he knew about my dad's problem with the Chinese government.

"I heard a rumor that you were climbers, which was confirmed the moment I saw you," Chin said.

"How did you know?" Alessia asked.

"Your hands."

We looked at our hands. They were all a little scarred, gnarled, and callused, with fingernails that hadn't grown back correctly after being torn off on some rockface, or in my case, on skyscrapers.

Chin held up his small manicured hands. They were in great shape, except for the two missing digits on his left hand. "My hands took a decade to heal," he said. "But of course the finger and thumb did not grow back. I lost them on Hkakabo Razi. My last climb. I assume that is why you are here."

We didn't respond.

Chin looked at Alessia. "I see that it is a secret. I am very good at keeping secrets."

"It's not exactly a secret," Ethan said. "We want to make the attempt without a lot of fuss, or distractions. We just want to climb."

"Completely understandable." Chin continued to look at Alessia. "You and I never saw each other here."

"My mother knows that I am traveling with Peak and Ethan, but she does not know that we have gone this far afield."

"I will keep your secret, but you must promise me something."

"What is the promise?"

"If any of you get into trouble, I want you to call me. I can be to you in a matter of hours. My pilot is a former Nepalese army pilot. He can land a helicopter almost anywhere and can fly at altitudes that helicopters are not supposed to reach."

"I promise," Alessia said. "And thank you."

"Good! Now we can talk openly about Hkakabo Razi.

Perhaps we should go back to the veranda and enjoy the night."

We sat around a teak table with the wind rustling the trees and the stream bubbling below.

"The mountain is responsible for my coming to Burma and obtaining the ruby I just showed you," Chin began. "When I was nineteen years old, our team attempted to summit Hkakabo Razi. The weather was good. We were camped at five thousand meters, well acclimated, and confident, ready to push for the summit early the next morning. As the youngest member of the team, I had gotten the worst tent site, at least ten meters from the other climbers. It had taken me hours to level out a spot beneath a small outcrop. After dinner with my teammates, I headed to my tent to get a few hours' sleep. It was a clear night with a million stars in the black, moonless, sky. I had a headlamp, but it was dim compared to what we have today. The slope was steep and icy. I had to use crampons and ice axes. If I slipped, it would be a two-hundred-meter slide to the bottom and a long climb back up—if I survived.

"Clearly, I was not paying as close attention to my path as I should have been. I was concentrating too much on how I was going to get there. I became disoriented. I knew I should have already reached my tent. It wasn't that far away. I looked back to where my teammates were camped, but could not see the lights from their tents. There was nothing but blackness."

I knew exactly what he was talking about. Night climbing can be terrifying. Even with a good headlamp, you can see no farther ahead than the beam. It's as claustrophobic as making your way through the jungle.

"I could have retraced my steps back to the team, woken them, and explained my dilemma." Chin smiled. "But of course as the youngest climber, I could not do this as it would have been too embarrassing. So I continued on my fruitless route until it occurred to me that I must be on the wrong path altogether. That I had started too low when I left the tents and had somehow passed below the shelf I had carved out. I climbed up the slope three meters, then started back the other direction, confident that I would find my tent." Chin closed his eyes. "That is when I heard a muffled thump, then a loud roar, like the sound of a fast train passing inches from my ears. I began to slide. I was tempted to use my axes to self-arrest, but I resisted the urge, hoping to stay ahead of the avalanche. But it caught me. I was buried alive in an icy grave for two days, frozen, many bones broken, drifting in and out of consciousness, waiting to die. Then a man appeared and saved me. He warmed me with his body for hours, then carried me down the mountain to a small village. I never learned his name. When he left, he said, "Now you must go out and do good things.""

Silence. What could we say after a story like that? The only sounds were moths clanking into the lanterns, attracted by their light, and the occasional skitter of lizards trying to catch them.

Not surprisingly, Ethan broke the silence. I was sure his legs were fidgeting beneath the table.

"What happened to the other climbers?"

"They are still on Hkakabo Razi."

This was followed by another long silence. Then Alessia said, "I did a great deal of research before we left for this climb. I did not read about this climb."

"That is because nothing was written about it, or even reported. My country, or former country, handles failure by pretending that it never happened. I was forbidden to speak about it, and until this moment I haven't. I broke my silence because I wanted you to know about the danger. Hkakabo Razi is a harsh and treacherous mountain."

"So you are Burmese now?" Nick asked.

"Yes, although I do still have my Chinese passport. I travel back and forth frequently. After I recovered from my injuries, which took some time, I knew my climbing days were over. I had a bit of family money and used it to travel with the vague idea of finding the man who had saved me. I heard that he was Tibetan, so I went to Tibet. I did not find him, nor did I find him in Nepal, nor in Thailand, India, or Bangladesh. He was the reason I traveled, but I suppose I was really searching for myself. I came to Burma for the simple reason that this is where I had recovered. The villagers told me that the man was not Burmese and had headed back north two days after he had left me. I did not find the man, but I did find the ruby. I paid the owner the last of my money for the gem. I sold it, and suddenly I was a businessman, an occupation that I had never contemplated. I cannot say that it has been completely fulfilling, but the profit has allowed me to do some good things."

"I noticed the guards on the roof," Ethan said.

Chin laughed. "You probably thought that I was a drug trafficker."

I flushed a little, because that's exactly what I had thought. I think all of us did.

"That is one thing I do not buy or sell. That would not be doing a good thing. But I will admit that I do sell gems to drug lords from time to time. I don't mind taking their money. The guards are here to protect the gems and the money I carry. This is not a good place if you have valuables in your possession. I am selling a large quantity of rubies. My buyer should be here tomorrow, or the next day. If you wish, I could give you a ride to the base of the mountain, although my helicopter is small—we might have to take two trips. But I don't mind. It would save you days of hardship."

If he had made this offer five days ago, I would have jumped up from the table and sprinted to the helicopter. Now I wasn't so sure.

"It's a kind offer," Nick said. "But I need to stay on the ground for my work." He looked at us. "But there is no reason why you three can't—"

"I think we would prefer to walk," Alessia said.

Ethan and I agreed.

TEN

"DEAD DONKEY," NICK SAID.

It had been a grueling trek, but none of us regretted forgoing Chin's helicopter. Alessia and I were drinking tea and waiting for our oatmeal to cook. I wasn't sure where Ethan was. He had gone off into the tangle right after he woke and hadn't come back yet.

"How did the donkey die?" Alessia asked.

"Broken neck. I think. Ran into a tree. Two of the porters saw it happen. The animals were foraging calmly. Then suddenly one bolted, hitting a tree trunk so hard a bird nest fell to the ground. It was the same donkey we had trouble with on the bridge. The porters said the donkeys had been a little skittish last night as if something was lurking in the forest."

"Tiger?" I asked.

"Unlikely, and even if it was a tiger, that doesn't account for the donkey bolting. The porters saw nothing that would make the donkey take off like that. We'll have to redistribute our gear, which means we'll be carrying more on our backs. In all the years I've been doing expeditions, this is the first time

I've had a pack animal die on me. If I'd been smart, I would have given my specimens to Chin to take back to Yangon. It would have saved a quarter of the load we're hauling."

"I think he was sincere about helping us if we were in trouble," Alessia said. "We could call him on the satellite phone."

"He's probably on the other side of the country by now. By trouble, I think he meant an emergency. A dead donkey is an inconvenience. But I've been considering Chin's orchid proposal the past couple of days. I think I went a little self-righteous on him. A few orchids would not collapse the ecosystem, and getting funding for expeditions is not easy. I'm paying for half this trip out of my own pocket. I think I objected because I thought he was in the drug trade, something I will never be part of."

So I wasn't the only one to have thought this. Ethan wandered back into camp.

"A donkey has died," Alessia said.

"I know. I saw it. I was looking for pugmarks."

"Pugmarks?" I asked.

"*Pug* is Hindi for 'foot,'" Alessia explained.

I wasn't surprised she knew this. Her father had been a wildlife conservationist. She had traveled all over the world with him. He had been murdered in the Congo by gorilla poachers when she was ten years old. She was our wildlife biologist. She had been able to identify all the mammals we had spotted, and nearly all the birds.

"I'd give anything to see a wild tiger," Ethan said. "Even a glimpse through the tangle would work. I didn't see anything except a fire with a half-eaten monkey on it. Kind of wish I hadn't seen that. Looked a little too human for my taste. I get that people need protein. But monkey? No thanks." He looked down at our boiling water. "What's cooking?"

"Oatmeal."

"I'll get my spoon. I'm starving."

Ethan didn't find his special spoon, which he had used to shovel food into his mouth on all seven continents. We left minus one donkey and one spoon, arriving at the next bridge with plenty of time to cross before dark. Except that the bridge was out. A group of people were standing on the opposite side of the deep ravine, looking down at the wreckage. Our side of the bridge was still anchored to trees.

"Is there another bridge across?" Alessia asked.

Nick pointed west. "A hard day's walk and another day to get back on track. And there is no guarantee that the bridge downriver will be up. This bridge is usually the best of the two. I guess this is where we part ways."

"What are you talking about?" I asked.

"The bridge," Nick said. "With the slats, it's almost like a ladder on this side. You won't have any problem getting down and across even with your heavy gear. See how it's draped over the river? It looks like a relatively easy climb on the other side for you, but not for the donkeys, or an old man whose climbing days are over. I'm certain you can hire people on the other side to porter you. They're stuck and would be happy to make money while they wait for the bridge to be repaired. I'm going to have to head downriver with the pack animals."

I looked over the edge. He was right. It would take a couple of extra trips, but it would be easy to get down to the river, even with our heavy gear. I estimated that each trip across would take us an hour, maybe a little more. There were now ten people standing across the ravine, including a couple little girls the two Peas' age. I could have no sooner stranded them than I could strand my twin sisters, whom I loved more than anyone in the world.

Chin's mysterious rescuer's words came back to me. *Now you must go out and do good things.* I desperately wanted to climb out of this simmering soup pot, but we had something good to do.

"I think we can fix it," I said.

SMILING FACES GREETED US when we finally reached the top of the opposite bank. There were more people stranded than I'd thought, thirty or forty. Most of them were traders carrying their wares on donkeys, or their backs. The two little girls who reminded me of the two Peas had gone shy on us now that we were face to face, hiding behind their parents' *longyi*s. The parents looked to be hauling all of their worldly possessions. I hoped they weren't moving to Strangeland. That was no place for kids.

The father of the girls introduced himself. His name was Yaza. From what we could tell from his broken English and Alessia's limited Burmese, the bridge had collapsed around midnight, dead-ending everyone who had arrived after dark.

Yaza took us over to the anchor trees. I expected to find rotted rope, but the ropes were fine. Yaza made a slicing motion with his hand. The ropes had been cut through with a sharp knife.

"Why?" Ethan asked.

"Runaway," Yaza answered.

"I don't understand."

"Bridge cut by person being chased. Cannot catch if no bridge."

Two men came out of the forest with heavy loads of stripped bark draped over their shoulders. They dumped the loads at the base of one of the anchor trees and started sorting through them.

"They make rope to fix bridge," Yaza explained.

While Alessia talked with Yaza's wife, Ethan and I walked back to the ravine and looked over the edge.

"What do you think?" Ethan asked. "They seem to be on top of this. Do you want to head north, or delay?"

"They're trying to rebuild it," I said. "We might be able to raise what's left with our gear. That would save them a lot of time."

Ethan nodded. "While we're alone, I have something else I want to talk to you about."

"Go ahead."

"Alessia told me this morning that she thinks the reason I want to climb Hkakabo Razi is so I'll get fired. Did she talk to you about that?"

"Actually, I talked to her about that. I don't know if her mother would fire you or not. I told her that you were probably getting restless."

"Am I that transparent?"

"Like aquarium glass."

Ethan grinned. "I gotta work on that. And you're right. I am getting a little antsy. Even if I don't get canned, I'm planning to move on. Alessia is perfectly safe in Yangon. I like hanging with her, but she doesn't need a full-time bodyguard. I've been teaching her mixed martial arts, and—don't tell her this—she's really good at it. So watch yourself. Don't cross her. She can kick your ass."

"I'll keep that in mind. Where are you going after this?"

"I was thinking about tagging along with you when you go to catch up with your dad."

"Love to have you, but by the time we finish, Josh's climb will be over. Getting back to Yangon might take us as long as it did to get here. We still have another bridge after this one. It might be out too."

"I've taken care of that. What I was doing this morning was looking for a hole in the canopy big enough to make a sat call. I talked to Chin for a couple of minutes. He said he'd be happy to give us a lift back to Yangon after we finish with Hkakabo Razi. We've already had our jungle experience. We don't need a repeat on the way back to make this climb legit. His chopper only holds four, but he thought he could squeeze in the three of us if we leave some gear behind."

"You'd leave your gear?"

"To forgo the jungle? In a minute. We'll get Thuta or someone to ship our gear back to the embassy. Alessia can ship it to wherever we end up."

"That means we have plenty of time to help them raise this bridge," I said.

"And the next bridge if the runner decides to take that one out too," Ethan added.

I can't describe the sense of relief and renewed energy I felt knowing we were not going to have to retrace our steps back through the tangle. Thanks to Nick, I had a better understanding and appreciation for the rainforest, but it still wasn't my favorite place.

We had plenty of rope to raise the bridge, but not enough to leave it behind, anchored to the tree. We explained this to Yaza. He passed it on to the others, who jumped into action by forming a rope assembly line. No one was idle. Even Yaza's girls were helping by carrying as much stripped bark as they could over their tiny shoulders.

Ethan had brought over not one, but two, continuous rope pulleys, or come-alongs. They are bulky and heavy. No alpine climber on earth carries a come-along, or two, in their gear bag. If I had seen them when we were desperately trying to lighten our load, I would have insisted that he leave them behind.

"Okay. I give up. Why did you bring these?"

"Ziplines," Ethan answered.

And that's what we used them for, to the amazement and amusement of the stranded travelers. We set up two ziplines, one on each side of the downed bridge. Once they were tight, we were able to zip across the ravine in a matter of seconds. We could lower ourselves down to the fallen bridge wherever we wanted without having to clamber across the slippery slats. I'm certain that, to the people watching us, we looked like spiders dangling from strands.

We were talking to each other about how best to raise the bridge, hanging maybe a foot above the water, when something hit Ethan's climbing helmet with a *pop* loud enough to be heard above the roaring river.

"Whoa!" Ethan said.

"Are you hurt?" Alessia asked.

"Just startled. That rock was moving."

I swung over and grabbed on to his harness to take a closer look at his helmet. There was a small crack in the yellow carbon shell.

"You're lucky it hit your helmet and not your head."

Ethan ran his finger over the crack. "I guess that's why we wear them."

I looked up. The only people watching us now were Yaza's girls. It was possible that they threw the rock, like kids do, and got lucky. Or unlucky. I waved at them. They waved back, then ran away.

"We need to get back to the problem at hand," Ethan said. "How are we going to raise this bridge?"

"I think the angle is too great to pull it up," Alessia said. "Perhaps we can salvage the planks and rope, then rebuild the bridge."

I was still looking up, thinking the girls might come back, when an idea for lifting the bridge came to me. "Or maybe we can change the angle of the pull," I said.

When we got back on top with my grand idea, we found that the stranded travelers had already figured out that the only way to raise the bridge was to change the angle. One of them had drawn a crude diagram in the dirt, which looked pretty much like what I had in mind. It was a heavy-duty platform made from trees sticking out from the rim. I had to smile. These people were far from helpless. This was not their first downed bridge, nor would it be their last. We might be able to save them a day or two with our gear, but no more than that. I sketched their plan into my notebook as they gave me advice over my shoulder. By the time I had it drawn to their satisfaction, it was dark.

Alessia and Ethan came into camp carrying our gear, having zipped back and forth with it while I sketched.

"Where's Nick?" The plan had been to bring him across on the zip.

"He decided to stay with the porters," Alessia said.

"More like he didn't want to jump into the dark abyss on a shoestring, as he called it," Ethan said. "Can't say I blame him. It was a little intense." He squatted down, looked at the sketch, and pointed at the pulleys. "I don't have any of those in my bag of tricks."

I showed him three wooden pulleys.

"Somebody had these?"

I shook my head. "They made them with their *panga*s and a dull chisel. They used a bent nail for the axle. They'll have three more ready by morning, which means we'll have three block and tackles. With your come-alongs and the scaffold, we can lift anything we want out of the ravine."

Yaza came over and invited us to dinner. We were given bowls of rice, dried fish, and chopsticks. I was about to ask the girls if they happened to toss a rock into the river earlier, but I didn't get a chance.

"My spoon!" Ethan said.

We only used spoons in camp among ourselves. When we ate with locals, we used chopsticks like they did.

"I thought you lost your—"

"The girl," Ethan said. "She's using my spoon."

I looked over at the girls. One of them was using a spoon to eat her rice. The other was using chopsticks. The camp was lit by a single lantern hanging from a tree. I didn't know how Ethan could say that it was his spoon. It was barely light enough to see that she was holding a spoon.

"She found it here last night near a campfire," Yaza said. "You were on this side last night?"

"No, I wasn't," Ethan said. "May I see it?"

Reluctantly, the girl handed the spoon to him. Ethan turned it over. Scratched into the underside were the initials *ET.*

"The last time I remember using the spoon is the night before the donkey died. I usually zip it in the right side pocket of my pack after I use it, so I don't lose it. It's possible I could have set it down on the log I was sitting on and someone came through camp while we slept and swiped it. But I'm pretty careful with my spoon."

He held the spoon out to the girl. She grabbed it.

ELEVEN

I'M GETTING MY MAGIC SPOON back before we leave," Ethan said. "I have some stuff I'm sure the girl will trade for. When I leave the French embassy, the only thing I'm taking with me is my magic spoon."

Alessia came out of her tent. "What is this talk about a magic spoon?"

"The spoon is magic," Ethan insisted. "How else could it have crossed the river on its own?"

"It was stolen," Alessia said. "Why is this spoon so important to you?"

Ethan's normally cheerful face turned serious. "My mother gave me the spoon the day I left for the corps. I know, kind of a weird gift, but it had belonged to a set passed down from my great grandmother. Sterling silver, mahogany box, red velvet interior. A complete set. Nothing missing. Mom didn't have much, but she had the silver. Just before I drove off for boot camp, she gave me the spoon and said, "Bring this back, son. Don't break up my silver set."

"Why did you not give it back to her?" Alessia asked.

"She died. Brain aneurysm while doing CrossFit. I was deployed overseas at the time."

"I am so sorry," Alessia said.

I felt really bad for him. I couldn't imagine losing my mom. This was the first time he had opened up to me. When we talked, it was always gear, mountains, and climbing. I'd never given a thought to his family. He had never mentioned them.

"I'm sorry too," I said, which seemed totally inadequate, as it always does.

"It's fine," Ethan said, waving us off. "It was a long time ago. I'm just trying to explain why I'm freaked out over the spoon."

"What about your father? Did you not want to bring the spoon back to him?" Alessia asked.

"By the time I got back from the Mideast, my dad had remarried. His new wife decided to get rid of my mom's stuff. The set was sold at a garage sale. I have a sister, two years younger than me. She said that the silver set sold for cheap because a spoon was missing."

"Where does your sister live?" I asked.

"DC. Works for a senator."

"Does she climb?"

"She's afraid of heights, and a lot of other things. She got my dad's genes. I got my mom's—she always pushed herself to her personal limits, which I guess is what got her in the end. She couldn't sit still."

On cue, Ethan got up and started pacing as he drank

his tea. When he finished, he dumped the dregs out and said, "I better find the girl before she trades my spoon to someone else. I bet there are fifty people here now. They're always swapping stuff."

I got up too. "Alessia and I will check on the rope makers."

"No," Alessia said. "I will talk to the girl. I doubt you have anything she will trade for your precious spoon."

Ethan and I walked up to where they were making rope. They must have worked through the night because there were dozens of yards of thick rope coiled on the ground like enormous pythons. Another group of men had cut down a couple of giant trees and were trimming and sizing them for the platform.

"I want to get my hands on one of those axes and see what that feels like."

While Ethan played lumberjack, I wandered around until I found Alessia. She was leaning against a tree near the ravine, holding Ethan's spoon in her hand.

"A necklace for the older girl," she said. "A bracelet for the younger girl."

"I think they got the better end of the deal."

"I think not. I have three sets of identical baubles, which I brought as gifts. All I had to do to make them look valuable was to wear them when I negotiated for the spoon."

Ethan walked up to us. "My spoon!"

OUR JOB WAS TO LOOSEN the planks snagged on the river rocks and make what repairs we could to the ropes holding the bridge together. It was hard and tedious work, made harder by being in harness, but the water running over the jagged boulder cooled the air to a tolerable temperature.

High above us, the men had already skidded two gigantic logs to the rim, positioned them so they were jutting out thirty feet over the river, and gotten busy lashing them together. Their next step was to brace the logs by building a scaffolding underneath.

"I'm going up to give them a hand!" I shouted above the roar of the rapids.

Alessia and Ethan gave me a wave. They were in the process of dislodging a very stubborn set of planks. I started jugging myself up to the zip with mechanical ascenders, or Jumars. The temperature seemed to rise every foot I gained. I had to rest and catch my breath every twenty feet. I was taking my final rest twenty feet from the zip when a rock hit me on the shoulder. It felt like a bullet. If I hadn't been in harness, it would have knocked me from the rope. My right arm went completely numb. My hand dropped from the ascender. Instinctively I hooked the rope with my foot to relieve the strain on my left hand. I was in no danger of falling onto the sharp river rocks, but I was risking a fall the length of my safety rope—jarring and painful, to say nothing about dangling upside down trying to regrab my ascenders. Below, Alessia and Ethan were shifting rocks. Above, men were roping together the bamboo scaffold. No one was paying the slightest attention to me. I could have shouted out, but I wasn't in enough trouble to warrant that kind of panic. Yet.

More debris fell from where they were building the scaffold, but none of it rained down as hard as the rock that had hit me. I tried to flex my right hand. I wasn't able to make a fist, but could move it, which was a good sign. I hoped it would get better after a little more rest. The foot I had wrapped around the rope started to tingle. I was going to have to readjust before it fell asleep. I managed to pull myself up just enough to switch feet. I was getting more feeling in my arm. I was able to make a loose fist. *Five more minutes, and I'll be fine,* I thought confidently, and that's when a man above dropped a load of bamboo. The load missed me by an inch, but it was hurtling down like spears aimed directly at the unsuspecting Alessia and Ethan.

"Above!" I shouted. "Above!"

Ethan and Alessia swung out of the way half a second before the bamboo shafts splintered on the rocks where they'd been standing. They waved. I waved back, forgetting that my right arm was injured. I don't think I screamed, but Alessia swears that I did. She was up her rope and next to me a full minute before Ethan, who may not have been the best climber I'd ever seen, but he was the fastest. I told Alessia about my shoulder. She told me I was a fool. When Ethan reached us, he said all three of us were fools for working directly beneath what amounted to the construction zone on an unstable wall. He climbed up to the zipline, clipped a rope to it, and with some effort, ratcheted me up.

Alessia scolded me the entire time she patched me up back at camp. I wasn't sure what she was saying, because she was speaking in rapid French, but her tone was clear.

Ethan walked up. "How's the wing?"

"Not broken, but it hurts."

"He will not let me put it into a sling," Alessia complained.

"Because he doesn't want it to stiffen up," Ethan said. "He's going to need two arms when we get to the mountain, which is going to be sooner than we thought. They're about ready to raise the bridge."

"I won't be much help with my bum arm."

"As it turns out, neither will I," Ethan said. "Come on."

We followed him to the ravine. Everyone was lined up along the edge, including Yaza, his wife, and their little girls, proudly wearing their new bling. I looked across the ravine and saw that there were almost as many watching on the other side as there were on this side, including Nick, who was easy to spot, being a foot taller than everyone else.

I looked downriver, expecting to see a dozen men manning ropes, but there were only two men standing some distance away from the bridges and the ropes they had set to raise it. The log platform jutting out over the edge was jammed with men tying rope around two gargantuan logs. It took me a while to figure out that they had no intention of pulling the bridge up. They were going to use gravity to lift it. This was not in the plans I had copied for them.

As soon as they had the ropes around the logs secured, all but two men left the platform and grabbed the ropes wrapped around the anchor trees. The two men on the platform positioned themselves next to the logs and, roughly at the same time, levered them over the edge. As the huge logs fell, the bridge snapped up from the river with planks clattering louder than the rapids. The anchor men quickly took up the slack around the trees and tied the ropes off.

The bridge was up.

TWELVE

NICK AND HIS PORTERS AND DONKEYS were the last to cross the bridge from the south early the next afternoon.

"How's your shoulder?" he asked.

"Stiff, but better." The shoulder was only marginally better. I had spent most of the day confined to camp, wandering over to check on the bridge construction, catching up on my journal, and swatting insects.

"Are you ready to travel?"

"I'll be good tomorrow morning."

"I meant now," Nick said.

I looked up through the trees. There were only a few hours of daylight left. Nick liked setting up camp long before dark.

"We still have the animals packed," he continued. "They're well rested, and so am I, for that matter, but if your shoulder—"

"No, I'm good," I said. "All I have to do is pack my gear."

"Alessia and Ethan are retrieving the climbing ropes and

will be along soon. There's another reason for us to be pushing on. I hesitate to mention it, because it's just a rumor, but Major Thakin might be back in the picture. The word is he's been asking about us. As far as I can determine, he's a day behind us."

"What does he want with us?"

Nick laughed. "I suspect he's found another irregularity in your travel permit and needs more cash to fix it. We have only one more bridge to cross before we reach the foothills of Hkakabo Razi. It will save you money if you start your climb before he arrives with his soldiers. They are not equipped for scaling a mountain. I've sent the porters ahead. I'll haul your pack to them."

"I can carry my own pack."

Nick shook his head. "That's already been decided. You have been outvoted three to one."

They were right. I couldn't carry a backpack. My shirt felt like too much weight. I stuffed my pack with gear while Nick collapsed my tent and rolled it up—something I would have had a hard time doing with one arm. When we were finished, Nick slipped the heavy pack over his shoulders and adjusted the straps.

"Just follow the hoof prints and look for our campfire. We'll keep it burning until you arrive."

"Thanks for carrying my load."

"No worries."

I watched him until he was hidden by the trees. The only things I had kept back were my water bottle, my headlamp, and my journal. I walked over to the ravine to give Alessia and Ethan a hand. Of course they wouldn't let me and even barred me from going out onto the bridge because I couldn't use both arms to balance myself. Except for Alessia and Ethan, everyone was gone. Once the ropes were unknotted and coiled, we returned to camp. I watched Alessia and Ethan pack until my guilt over doing nothing to help took me to the trail to look for donkey hoof prints, which turned out to be easy to find. The trail was clear, but boggy from the foot traffic leading down to the bridge from the north. It would be a difficult uphill slog. I returned to camp, where Alessia informed me that she was going to tape my arm to my side so I didn't swing it while I walked. I got out of the mummy treatment by promising to keep my right hand in my pocket.

"But if I see you wince one time," Alessia said, "I will pin your arm, or wing, as Ethan calls it."

"Deal."

Ethan led the way. A half mile out, we came to a steep hillside with slippery switchbacks that did not seem to have an end. Alessia and Ethan stopped and pulled out their trekking poles. My poles were in my pack somewhere ahead. Not surprisingly, Ethan had a spare set and offered them to me.

"He is only allowed to use one of the sticks," Nurse Alessia said.

Reluctantly, I handed one of the poles back to Ethan. "Are you still hauling those heavy come-alongs?"

Ethan grinned. "I wish I was. We might need them to get up this hillside. I traded them for a donkey to replace the one Nick lost. It wasn't the best deal I've ever made. The donkey was ancient, but Nick was grateful to have it."

The sun set behind the hill, and the forest went dark. Unburdened, I easily took the lead. A few yards ahead of them, I took my right hand out of my pocket, fully expecting Alessia to shout at me or, worse, wrap me up, but she said nothing. She either hadn't noticed or she was too exhausted to care. My shoulder felt a little better now that I was moving it. The constant throbbing faded to a dull ache, interrupted by sharp stabs of pain every hundred steps, which I could live with.

The trail was three feet wide, with a sheer drop off on the right or the left, depending on the direction of the switchback. I concentrated on the ten-foot swatch of headlamp light and muddy tracks in front of me. Rain dripped through the canopy, frogs jumped across the trail, insects dined on me— which I ignored because I couldn't swat them with my right hand and I had a pole in my left. There was no way that Nick could set up camp along here. He had either pitched his tent on top of the hill or at the bottom on the other side. I had looked at Nick's topo map a couple of nights earlier. We had to traverse several giant hills like this before we reached Hkakabo Razi. From the top of one of the hills, we would get our first glimpse of the snow-covered peak.

I glanced back to check for Alessia's and Ethan's headlamps. They had fallen way behind. In fact, they were on the switchback below me. I stopped so they could catch up. I knew I had been walking fast because I was a little out of breath. I unhooked my water bottle from my gear belt. As I put it to my lips, I had the distinct feeling that someone, or something, was watching me. I recapped the bottle without taking a sip. I wondered if it was one of those feelings Zopa was always talking about. *The unseeable that lurks on the fringe of our perception. Like tiny spiders on our back. You can see it if you quiet your mind.*

I took a deep breath, let it out slowly, then looked again. Alessia and Ethan had rounded the corner and were headed directly toward me, maybe a hundred yards away, their head-lamps bright in the darkness. I made a slow turn in place and stopped halfway around. It wasn't a tiny spider. It was a tiger. The big cat was standing fifty feet away, its yellow eyes locked on me. He was carrying what looked like a small muntjac, or barking deer, in his mouth. We had seen several of the little deer during our trek. I willed myself to stand completely still. I was more stunned than I was afraid. The tiger's fur was damp with rain. Ethan's and Alessia's lights were getting brighter, dancing on the trees. I didn't warn them. The tiger was not a threat, and even if he was a threat, there was nothing we could do to stop it.

"Thanks for waiting!" Ethan shouted from behind.

I glanced at them. When I turned back, the tiger was gone.

"Tiger," I said.

"No way!" Ethan said. "Where?"

I pointed up the trail.

"That's why I don't like being the caboose. By the time you come along, all the good stuff in front has been scared off. How big was it?"

"Big. An adult."

"How long was it there?"

"A few seconds, but felt like an hour. He was carrying a dead muntjac in his mouth."

"Aw, man! Are you serious?" Ethan went ahead to check for pugmarks.

"That must have been remarkable to see," Alessia said.

"It was. I wish you had seen it."

"I too wish." She touched my right arm. "It is not in your pocket."

"I know. It was too hard to balance on the slippery trail." I gently rotated my shoulder. It stung, but it wasn't bad.

"Perhaps you should use two poles now."

"I think I'll stick with one. It seems to be working."

"Pugmarks!" Ethan said.

We joined him. He was crouching over several very large tiger prints in the soft mud. He held his index finger up. It was bloody.

"Muntjac blood," I said.

"I still can't believe I missed the cat. The pugmarks went up the bank, so there's a chance we might see the tiger again on a higher switchback."

In the dark, it was impossible to tell how far up the hillside we had traveled. We'd been walking for hours. The next switchback might be our last.

"I'll take the lead," Ethan said, and started off.

Alessia and I followed at a much slower pace. I asked her if she had ever seen a tiger in the wild. She had been interested in the pugmarks, but not overly excited.

"Yes. When I was a little girl in India with my father. He tranquilized three from elephant back and put radio collars around their necks to study their movements."

"So, riding Nagathan was not your first time on elephant back?"

"No. And it was not nearly as comfortable as the elephants we rode in India. It is good to know there is at least one tiger left in Burma. I will write to my father's colleagues when we return home."

Ethan had already started walking up the next switch-back. His headlamp was moving toward us now.

"It seems he is, how do you say it? Ditching us. Not leading."

"He'll stop if he sees the tiger or pugmarks."

"But he will not continue working at the embassy," Alessia said sadly. "He told me he was going away with you when we return to Yangon, regardless of whether my mother fires him or not. Which my mother would never do. She trusts him. She knows I will climb with or without him. She would prefer that he climbs with me. I was wondering . . ." She hesitated.

"Go ahead."

"I was wondering, if it is agreeable to my mother, and I am certain it will be. I was thinking that I would like to accompany you and Ethan when you visit your father. I have always wanted to meet him."

Everyone wants to meet Joshua Wood until after they've actually met him. He is great-looking, smart, charming, a world-class climber, and a flake. Don't get me wrong. I love my dad, but he has never really been there for me. Even when he bailed me out of the jam I'd gotten myself into in New York, he was helping me to help myself. It hadn't worked out for him, because I hadn't taken the final few steps to the summit of Everest. I still wasn't sure why I hadn't taken those steps. Was it for Sun-jo and his sisters? Was it for Sun-jo's father, who had died saving Josh's life on K2? Was I punishing Josh for not being there for me and for using me? It was complicated.

"So, you do not think it is a good idea," Alessia said.

"No, no." I took her hand. "It's a great idea. I was just thinking about my dad. He'll really like you."

She gave me a bright smile.

"But first we have to run him to ground."

"Run him to ground?"

"Find out where he is."

"And we have to climb Hkakabo Razi."

"It won't be long now. I already feel the chill in the air."

"Really?"

I laughed. "No, not really."

"Do you know what I feel?" She leaned toward me. Our lips touched. Just for a second, then she leaned back. "What I feel is your hand gripping mine as if there is no problem whatsoever."

She was right. I didn't feel any pain whatsoever.

"Do you want me to carry your pack?"

"No," she said firmly.

"Pugmarks!" Ethan shouted from the switchback above.

THIRTEEN

THERE WERE THREE MORE SWITCHBACKS. Pugmarks across all of them. The tiger had taken a shortcut, bounding straight uphill carrying its kill. Even though the cat was long gone, I still had the spidery feeling we were being watched. When we reached the top, the rain really started coming down, along with lightning, crashing thunder, and wild wind. We walked, or slid, our way down the other side in ankle-deep water and oozing sludge, getting to Nick's camp just shy of midnight.

Nick was sitting next to the fire in a rain poncho, keeping the fire alive. The porters had built a rope corral at the edge of camp and were all asleep on the ground, wrapped in tarps, while the donkeys huddled near a tree, ears pinned to their heads, trying to stay out of the rain.

"Wasn't sure if you would make it tonight or not," Nick said. "Nasty weather, but it will blow out soon. We corralled the donkeys so they wouldn't get smashed by windfalls. Lucky we did, because we had a visitor a couple hours ago."

"A tiger?" Ethan asked.

"How did you know?"

"Was it carrying a muntjac?" I asked.

"It was carrying something when it streaked through, but I couldn't tell what it was."

I told him about my brief encounter on the trail.

"My guess is that it was a male tiger carrying dinner home to his mate and cubs. That is fabulous, but we need to keep this sighting among ourselves. Don't even tell the porters. Luckily they were tucked in for the night when the tiger passed through here. Word will get out soon enough, bringing in poachers from hundreds of miles away to kill and part the cat out. We were lucky to see it. I'm concerned that it had no fear of us. Someday it will stop on a trail to gaze at a hunter with a rifle, and that will be the last human the tiger sees."

With that pretty image, I pitched my tent, crawled inside, and fell asleep to the sound of heavy rain.

I woke at dawn to the call of birds, the buzz of insects, and the rustle of donkeys in the makeshift corral. I crawled out of my tent. The wet ground was misty from the cool rain. It looked like I was the first one up. Even the porters were still wrapped in their tarps, looking like colorful giant grubs. I stretched and found I could lift my right arm above my head with only a small jolt of pain.

"Shoulder's better," Ethan said.

I turned around and looked at his yellow tent. The flap was zipped closed. I didn't see him anywhere.

"Up here," he said.

I looked up. I still didn't see him.

"Here."

His head was sticking out of a camouflaged tent made out of mosquito netting perched in a tree ten feet above the ground.

"You spent the night up there?"

"Yeah, couldn't sleep. I've been wanting to try this thing, but didn't find the right tree until last night. The top is waterproof, and I have a sweet little hammock. The sway from the wind took some getting used to. It wasn't much different from sleeping in a portaledge on a wall, but the fall is a lot shorter and the ground is a lot softer if you get unhooked in the night."

"What else do you have in your magic backpack?"

He put his head back into the tent, then poked it out wearing a pair of goggles that made him look like a big insect emerging from a knothole.

"What are those things?"

"Night vision goggles."

He rolled out of the tent, dangled from the branch for a moment, then dropped to the ground like a gymnast sticking a perfect landing. He took the goggles off and handed them to me.

"I really wanted to see that tiger. I thought he might drop the muntjac off and pass through here again on his way back to the grocery store."

"Did he?"

"I'm not sure. Batteries went dead after a couple of hours, but I did see something."

"What?"

"A ghost."

"I don't believe in ghosts," I said.

"Yeah, me either. Let's take a look."

I followed him over to the edge of the clearing, where he squatted down and started examining the ground.

"What are you looking for?"

"Footprints."

"I don't think ghosts leave footprints."

"Exactly. There!" He pointed at a shallow depression in the mud. It didn't look like a footprint to me. It could have been anything. "One over here."

I looked. It was another nondescript depression.

"Ah, here we go. Pugmark."

It wasn't a tiger print unless the tiger was wearing sandals, and none of us were wearing sandals. We were all wearing waterproof hiking boots so our feet wouldn't rot off our ankles.

"I had this weird feeling that we were being followed or watched last night," I said.

"Me too. I didn't say anything because I thought I was being paranoid. An occupational hazard from being in the corps. When you spotted the tiger, I thought that maybe that was what was giving me the jitters."

"Maybe this print belongs to one of the porters."

Ethan shook his head. "I don't think so. They were all wrapped up for the night. They're all wearing tennis shoes. And I recognized the peeping Tom."

"Who was it?"

"Lwin."

"Lwin is dead."

"Apparently not."

I stared down at the footprint, remembering Lwin's tattered sandals. I hadn't paid any attention to the tread. Why would I? I hadn't paid any attention to what the porters' foot-wear was either.

"They found Lwin's body," I said.

"They found a couple of small pieces of a body and what looked like Lwin's *longyi.*"

"If the pieces weren't Lwin's, whose were they?"

"I don't know. So, your shoulder's better?"

"I think it's fine."

"You're lucky Lwin didn't hit you in the face or neck."

"Come on! Lwin is . . ." I thought about it for a moment. "Your helmet?"

Ethan nodded. "That rock hit pretty hard. Too hard for a falling rock, or someone hurling it at me from the top of the ravine. When you got bulleted in the shoulder, it was too big of a coincidence. And the donkey that died? It was the same one that bolted on the bridge. The same one that Lwin tried to *panga* to death after it kicked him. I started thinking about Lwin's so-called death and the fact that he popped his girlfriend with a slingshot. When they found Lwin, they didn't find his bag. One of the soldiers might have found our cash inside and swiped it, but why not just take the cash and bring the bag in as evidence? Lwin carried his *panga* and slingshot strapped around his waist within easy reach. I'm sure it was a mess, but they should have found something besides Lwin's gaudy *longyi.* A soldier wouldn't have stolen the slingshot or the *panga.* They'd have no interest in those primitive weapons. If Lwin set up his own death, he would need the slingshot and the *panga* so he wouldn't actually die in the forest after he'd allegedly died."

In a weird way, Ethan's scenario made sense. What didn't make sense was Lwin sticking around to take potshots at us with the major on his trail, which he had to know about. If he was alive, he must be the runner who had cut the bridge. And why was he harassing us? We had done Lwin a favor by paying him full price for half the trip.

"Why would he risk getting caught by following us around?" I asked.

Ethan shrugged. "No idea. And consider this. There's a possibility that he didn't have anything to do with the guy's murder in the forest. The victim might have simply gotten too close to Nagathan. I think that Nagathan would have killed us too if we had strayed within reach. Lwin might have seen the carnage and decided to exploit the guy's death."

"So you're sure it was Lwin."

"Not one hundred percent. The goggles aren't that good. They're a little fuzzy, and of course you don't see things in color. But the pattern of the *longyi* matched Lwin's. Those little snake things. I haven't seen another like it out here, and Lwin had at least two other *longyi*s just like it in his kit."

That didn't mean that someone else wasn't wearing the same pattern *longyi*, but it was an odd coincidence.

"He was squatted out here for a half hour or so," Ethan continued. "I thought about grabbing him, but I knew he'd be long gone before I could get to him. Nick came out of his tent with a flashlight to take a pee. Lwin knew enough to stay in place. He got up as soon as Nick was zipped back into his tent. He stood there for a couple of minutes, listening, I guess, then turned and walked into the trees.

"I don't know if you noticed, but Lwin had a strange gait.

It wasn't exactly a limp, but his right foot kind of swung out a little every time he took a step. I meant to ask him about it, but I didn't get a chance. My guess is that he broke the leg when he was young and it didn't heal right. He didn't exactly favor it, but whatever happened changed his natural stride."

I hadn't noticed anything about Lwin's gait, natural or unnatural, nor had I paid any attention to Ethan's acute observational skills. I guess his restlessness disguised the fact that he was paying close attention to those around him.

"I think Lwin will cut the next bridge before Major Thakin gets here, if he hasn't cut it already," Ethan said. "He didn't appear to be carrying anything, which means he can travel fast. I think that monkey on the fire I found a few days ago was Lwin's leftover dinner. The jungle is a well-stocked grocery store if you aren't picky about what you eat. Speaking of which, I think he swiped my spoon, found out it wasn't good for eating roasted monkey, and left it."

I grimaced, thinking of all the horrible things I'd seen Lwin gobble down.

"I guess we should wear our climbing helmets everyplace we go," I said.

"Not a bad idea, but that might tip our hand. You say your shoulder's good?"

"Yeah."

"Can you haul your pack?"

"I think so."

"Good. It's my turn to have the donkey carry my load."

"We're taking turns?"

"No, but I can't shadow you with a pack on my back. The only way to protect you and Alessia from Lwin is to get eyes on him. I'm going to have to go back to Force Recon mode. Lwin is pretty sneaky, but I'm sneakier."

Force Reconnaissance are the marines who go behind enemy lines to gather intelligence before the main force arrives.

"And what will you do if you get eyes on him?"

"That's entirely up to Lwin. If you're asking if I'm going to kill him, the answer is probably not. All he's done is hurl a couple of rocks at us. But I am going to find out why he's following us and put a stop to it."

Ethan didn't mention how he was going to find out without speaking Burmese and Lwin not speaking English. He crawled into his tent and came out a few minutes later dressed from head to toe in camo, including green and black smears of greasepaint on his face.

"I can't see you," I joked.

"That's the point. Will you pack my gear?"

"Sure."

"Don't forget my tree tent. See you at the final bridge."

He vanished into the misty forest.

FOURTEEN

"DO YOU SEE HIM?" ALESSIA ASKED.

"No, do you?"

"No."

"We're not supposed to see him. Ethan is watching Lwin. If Lwin is watching us, Ethan is close by, watching Lwin."

I tried to get away with telling Alessia and Nick that Ethan had decided to forge ahead on his own and would meet us at the bridge. I'm not a very good liar. They stared at me in silence for several seconds, which was all it took for me to spill my guts. Nick was of the opinion that Lwin was an apparition and that ghosts could not use slingshots.

"The forest is filled with spirits and ghosts," he said. "I'm surprised it took Ethan this long to spot one."

This was a little shocking coming from a scientist. When I asked him about this, he smiled and said, "Boo! Mate."

Alessia, like Ethan and me, didn't believe in ghosts either, but she did admit that Lwin had made her uncomfortable. I suggested that she wear her helmet.

"Only if you wear yours."

So, we were both walking ahead of Nick and the porters, sweating in our helmets, which were as hot as pressure cookers.

Up and down we trudged, with the only upside being that we would be in terrific shape when we finally reached Hkakabo Razi. My legs were not the only things that were getting stronger. Nick didn't care if Lwin was alive or a ghost. There were trees to climb and specimens to be collected. My shoulder was still a little stiff, but the more I climbed, the better it felt. Alessia and I explored the same trees. She on one side, me on the other, meeting in the middle every few feet to show each other what we had discovered. This is how I thought it was going to be before I came to Burma. Just Alessia and me exploring together, hanging out (literally in this case), getting to know each other.

We climbed a behemoth tree a hundred yards down from one of the switchbacks. Halfway up, we dispensed with our helmets. Lwin couldn't possibly hit us at this height through the dense foliage. When we reached the top, we found dozens of beautiful orchids. Purple, yellow, and red. Alessia picked a few and put them in her collection bag. I picked one and put it in her hair, which she had braided that morning and pinned to keep it away from her face.

We sat on a branch side by side swaying in the midst of orchids, knowing that we should climb back down, but not wanting to leave. Alessia was facing north, and I was facing south.

"Look!" Alessia said.

I turned. The sun had burned away the mist to the north, revealing a snow-covered peak.

"Hkakabo Razi," she said.

"It might be. There are more peaks to the west still covered by clouds. But it is beautiful, whatever peak it is."

"I want to be cold again," Alessia said. "I want to shiver."

This was the only time I had heard her even hint at being uncomfortable in the heat of the rainforest. Not once had she complained as we sat around the campfire after a long day's walk picking bloated leeches off each other's backs. Ethan and I whined like dogs during this disgusting process.

"I thought you liked the rainforest."

She shook her head so vigorously the orchid fell from her head. She caught it deftly, gave it a kiss, then slipped it under a hairclip so it wouldn't fall so easily.

"The rainforest, or the tangle, as you name it, is a means to an end." She pointed at the mountain. It was being overtaken by a fast-moving dark cloudbank, which meant high winds, and possibly snow. "Let's go down so we can get to that end."

Nick admired Alessia's orchid, saying that he had seen only two of them in his many years of collecting. He pointed at the tree. "And both times, they were found in a tree like this, growing on a steep hillside. It's an interesting find and very pretty in your beautiful hair."

"I can give you this one as well."

"Good lord, no! It belongs right where it is." He pointed. "Did you notice that we are going to have company?"

Across the valley to the north was a line of thirty or so people, single file, making their way down the switchbacks to the valley floor. They were too far away to see clearly, but judging by their slumped posture, they were carrying heavy loads.

"Traders and their porters?" Alessia asked.

"We'll find out soon enough. And if we don't get to the bottom before them, we will have a major traffic jam. This trail is a one-way road, especially with pack animals hauling wide panniers."

We got to the valley floor long before the others. Running along the valley was a crystal clear creek with a log across it. Lwin would have needed a chainsaw to take it out.

"This is the last bridge?" Alessia asked.

Nick shook his head. "The last bridge is on the other side of this hill. This is just a log across a little stream. We'll camp on the other side. There's no chance of our getting to the next valley before dark."

I was happy to stop for the day. By the time the other group arrived, we had set up camp, built our cooking fires, bathed downstream, and had water boiling for rice and tea.

Five exhausted Japanese climbers stumbled into camp as we were dishing out the rice. I recognized one of them, but couldn't remember his name. I had met him briefly on Everest the previous year.

"Peak Wood," he said, giving me a small bow.

At least he had gotten the first name right. I explained that I used my mother's last name, not my father's. He apologized profusely. I told him it was a common mistake and no big deal. But it kind of was a big deal because it was the first time anyone had called me Peak Wood. Josh had not raised me. I barely knew him. Nick and Alessia were giving me strange looks, and I'll admit it was a little strange to bring up the surname issue to a wiped-out climber in the middle of the jungle. He said his name was Hiro Yamada, then introduced the other four climbers.

"Your friend came out of the forest and nearly scared us to death," Hiro said. "He was disguised as a tree."

We all laughed, although I don't think Hiro was trying to be funny.

"He said to tell you that he was going to the bridge to make sure Lwin did not cut it down."

"Where did you see him?" I asked.

"Traveling downhill toward the bridge."

"Did you see anyone else on the other side?" Alessia asked.

"No one."

"Did you climb Hkakabo Razi?" Nick asked.

"Yes, but we did not summit. Conditions were bad. We made two attempts. It is a very difficult peak. We would have attempted a third time, but our supplies were too low and we were depleted from the first two attempts."

I was both happy and upset to hear this. We still had a shot at being the first climbers to measure the height with a GPS. But if Hiro hadn't been able to summit, what were our chances? He and his team were elite, world-class climbers. We were pretty good climbers, but not in their league.

"Are you climbing Hkakabo Razi?" Hiro asked.

"We are going to try," Alessia said.

Hiro nodded. I appreciated that he didn't break out in a belly laugh. He turned and said something in Japanese to his team members. Each of them responded with a slight nod. He turned back to us.

"We will camp on the other side of the stream. If you are interested, we will be happy to share what we have learned about Hkakabo Razi. Our maps and satellite photos were very different from the terrain we encountered on the climb. If I were to try again, I would approach the summit very differently."

"That is very generous of you," Alessia said.

Hiro bowed. "I was the climb master on Kilimanjaro for the Peace Climb. Sebastian Plank told me what happened to you in the Pamirs."

The billionaire, Sebastian Plank, had put young climbers on mountains all over the world for his Peace Climb documentary, paying for all the expenses. My stepfather, Rolf, who is one of Plank's attorneys, thinks the climbs had cost Plank eighty million dollars. I wasn't surprised that Hiro had been one of the climb masters, but I was surprised that Plank had told him what happened to us in the Pamirs. I was going to change the subject, but Hiro stopped me with a single word.

"Aki," he said.

Aki was the Japanese climber on our Pamir team. The *A* in *peace*, the summit of our failure along with Phillip, Elham, Choma, and Ebadullah.

AKI

ELHAM   CHOMA

PHILLIP   EBADULLAH

All of them murdered.

"Aki was my nephew," Hiro said.

This explained why Plank had told him about the Pamirs. Plank had personally accompanied the dead climbers back to their homes in his private jet and apologized to the families, even though none of their deaths were his fault. Their deaths were the fault of the men who had murdered them. I hadn't gotten to know Aki very well. He had paired off with Choma from the Ukraine the first day we were there, just as I had paired off, or tried to pair off, with Alessia. That's how it works in climbing. You pick someone, and if you get along, you stick with them for the entire climb.

"I am very sorry for your loss," Alessia said. "I wish I'd had the chance to know him better."

Hiro nodded. "No need to feel bad. The only reason I brought it to your attention was to explain how I knew about what happened to you in the Pamirs. When you climb a mountain, you need to be looking forward not backward."

I had to smile. His last sentence was so Zopa-like, I wondered if they had met up on Everest.

Hiro asked, "Would you like to meet at our camp, or shall we meet over here?"

"Why don't you join us for dinner here?" Nick offered.

"With my team?"

"Yes, of course. We have plenty of food."

Hiro gave another bow. "We will return as soon as we have set up our camp."

They returned with hand-drawn maps, videos, digital photos detailing different routes to the summit of Hkakabo

Razi. After a summit failure, every climber I know does a do-over of the climb in their minds for the next time, even if there isn't going to be a next time. I still think back to climbs that I failed when I was eight years old, wishing I could try them again, knowing, at least in my head, where I screwed up. What climbers do not do is share this information to help other climbers succeed where they failed.

Hiro and his team handed us the summit on a platter with firsthand information less than a week old. Within minutes, it was clear that our crude summit plan would not have worked. The maps we had were terribly inaccurate. It was as if they depicted a completely different mountain.

"There are several spires below Hkakabo Razi," Hiro said. "You must top all of them to reach the ridge to the summit."

One of the other climbers said something to Hiro, and pretty soon the conversation got a little heated as they flipped through notes, maps, photos, and videos on their five tablets. We, of course, didn't have a tablet between us, having left all of our gadgets back at the embassy. The team debate, or argument, came to an end, and Hiro turned to us.

"I am sorry for that," he said. "My team has brought forward an alternative route, which may have the potential of saving you a day, or two. I must caution you, though, that it is an untested route. It may even be a dead end, but if we were to make another attempt, we would seriously consider it. It could save time, or it might lose time. Fifty-fifty."

Climbing a new route is always fifty-fifty. Even if you are climbing a well-known route, there is a huge chance of failure because mountains are constantly changing.

Hiro flipped through several photos, stopping on a steep snowfield dotted by their bright alpine tents.

"This is our Camp One," he began, and for the next hour, we were given what amounted to a step-by-step narration of their attempt to summit Hkakabo Razi.

FIFTEEN

I've been up for hours. Alessia and Nick are asleep in their tents. Hiro has kindly lent me his tablet for the night so I can study it.

One thing we haven't discussed during this impulsive expedition is who is going to actually lead the climb. We don't need a leader here in the rainforest, but on the mountain, someone is going to have to call the shots. I'm not volunteering for the position, but I am thinking about who should fill this role as I slap insects writing this.

I'm probably the most experienced climber among the three of us, but Alessia isn't far behind. She has drive. This climb was her idea. And she is way more adaptable than Ethan and me. She always goes with the flow, no matter how torrential it is. What she lacks is an edge. Hiro appears to have it. Josh definitely has it. Every climb leader I have ever met has an edginess to them. I don't have an edge, not yet anyway, and neither does Ethan. He's a lot older than Alessia and me, but he's more of a blunt instrument than a sharp razor. He's a good climber, but he came to climbing later in life, using it as a means of doing something wacky like snowboarding down McKinley with wolves at his heels.

I'm beginning to think that none of us has the skills to lead our little team, and looking down at the photos, I'm beginning to think that we shouldn't climb Hkakabo Razi at all.

As we struggled through the tangle, I thought the reason people didn't try to summit the mountain was because it was so difficult to get to. Now that I've seen the photos and videos, I've realized that this isn't true.

My best climbing skill is not climbing. It's figuring out how to climb something. A weird way to look at the world, but I've been doing it since I was five years old. When we lived in Wyoming, Mom would be driving us somewhere, then suddenly leave the highway in our four-wheel-drive truck to bump over a washboard track for miles. She would stop in the middle of nowhere, grab her binoculars, and scan a nasty-looking cliff or a towering rock formation.

"Climb it," she'd say.

She didn't mean for me to actually climb, although I would have if she'd let me. She wanted me to plan a route to the top and explain it to her. If I made a mistake in the imagined climb, she wouldn't tell me where I had gone wrong. She would tell me to try again. Sometimes over and over, until I got it right. If it got dark before I figured it out, we would leave and come back the next day, or several days in a row, until I had done it. She didn't allow me to take a photo of the problem, insisting that my eyes were better than a camera lens and my brain was a better recording device. When we got back to our cabin, I would sketch what I remembered and stare at the drawing for hours. At night I would lie in bed with my eyes closed, visualizing the route and imagining myself climbing it. We argued about routes constantly. Eventually she let me try my routes out, which gave me a better idea of how to plan a climb from a distance.

When Mom married Rolf, we moved to New York, where I shifted from rocks to skyscrapers. I'd pick a building and look at it for weeks from every angle, at different times of day and night, until I figured out the best way to top it. People walking by me on the busy streets thought I was homeless. If I left my baseball cap on the ground in front of me, some of them would drop money into it. I should have explained that I wasn't panhandling (Rolf had plenty of money, and he was generous with it), but I said nothing and redistributed the wealth to those who needed it on my way back to our loft.

I had no intention of actually climbing the skyscrapers I studied. It was an exercise for a country kid who had nothing else to do in the big city. But the imagined climbs turned into an obsession, which led me to climbing the buildings, which led me to jail, which led me to Everest, which led me to the Pamirs, which led me to Alessia, which led me to the campfire I'm sitting at in the middle of nowhere, trying to figure out a route to the summit of Hkakabo Razi and . . .

SIXTEEN

A BUDDHIST MONK STEPPED OUT of the dark forest, his saffron-colored robe glowing in the dim light of the campfire. I nearly jumped out of my boots and dropped my journal into the fire, retrieving it a second before it ignited.

Zopa laughed.

Seeing him standing there was as likely as seeing Lwin's ghost or the tiger.

"Are your words burnt?"

I looked down at my journal. It was a little singed, but intact.

"What are you doing here?"

"Is there rice?"

"Yeah, but . . ."

He pulled a begging bowl and a pair of chopsticks out of his robe. "Good. I am hungry. Tea?"

There was little use in pushing Zopa for information at this point. He would tell me what he wanted me to know when he wanted me to know it. I put a pot of water on the fire for tea and asked if he wanted his rice warmed. He did. As I set the rice pot over the flames, he sat down in one of Nick's camp chairs and pointed at our tents. "From the Pamirs?"

I nodded.

"Good tents."

At the monastery in Kathmandu, he kept his head shaved, but there was a couple weeks of growth now, which meant he hadn't been at the monastery in a while. Where had he come from? Why was he here? How did he find me?

I prodded the fire with a stick as the rice warmed. When it was ready, I filled his bowl and handed it to him, then made the tea while he ate. As he sipped his tea, he pointed at the tablet next to my journal.

"The Japanese?"

"Yes. On loan. How did you know?"

"The Japanese always have the best electronics. I heard on my way here that they had a bad climb on Hkakabo Razi." He picked up the tablet. "Show me how this works."

I showed him, but it was clear that he already knew how *this* worked by the way he expertly flipped through photos and watched the short videos.

Josh described Zopa as cagey. He said that you never knew what his real motivation was for doing something. Zopa is a mystery, which is why I'm so fond of him. I decided to be mysterious too by not asking him any questions about his shocking appearance. I wanted to see how that felt.

After he finished flipping through the images, he got up from the chair and stretched. "I am very tired. I will sleep in Ethan's tent."

"Okay."

I didn't ask him how he knew Ethan wasn't inside the tent. He'd let me know soon enough. I had pitched the tent in case Ethan came back in the middle of the night. Zopa knew it was Ethan's tent because he had an identical one. It was part of the Plank gear from the Pamirs. All the support staff had been given yellow gear to distinguish them from the climbers. I wondered what Zopa had done with his expensive yellow gear, but I didn't ask. He probably sold it in Kathmandu and gave the money to the monastery. When he got to Ethan's tent, he turned and gave me a little wave and a smile.

THE HEAT INSIDE MY TENT WOKE ME. I looked at my watch groggily.

Crap!

It was 10:40. I sat up, quickly dressed, and crawled out. Nick and the porters were gone. So were the Japanese. Alessia was sitting on her pack reading a book near the fire. She smiled.

"Sleepyhead."

I attempted to smooth down my sweaty tent hair. "When did Hiro leave?"

"Hours ago."

"I need to give back his—"

"I gave it back to him," Alessia said. "You did not even stir when I took it from your tent."

I poured myself a cup of tea. "What are you reading?"

She held the book up. "*Stranger in a Strange Land* by Robert Heinlein."

"So, that's where you got the name for the village."

"Yes, I do love reading science fiction."

I did too. Her copy was mildewed and bloated. She was going to have to finish it soon before it disintegrated. I'd have to wait until I got home to read it.

"What time did Ethan get back?" Alessia asked.

"He's back?" I looked around camp.

"In his tent," Alessia said. "Snoring."

"Ethan doesn't snore."

Zopa wasn't snoring either. Not anymore anyway. He crawled out of his tent.

Alessia screamed in delight and surprise.

SEVENTEEN

"ETHAN WAS DRESSED LIKE A SHRUB," Zopa said. "I saw him on the other side of the bridge."

"He is guarding the bridge so it does not get cut down," Alessia said.

I told him about our troubles with Lwin as we climbed the steep trail.

"So," he said, "Ethan is a troll guarding a bridge from a rock-throwing ghost."

"Ball bearings, and they were real enough," I said, feeling a twinge of pain in my shoulder.

"Tell me about the botanist."

This explanation lasted all the way to the top of the hill, where we were greeted by a magnificent view of Hkakabo Razi. Nick had sent the porters on ahead and was talking to three men heading south. When the men saw Zopa, they dropped their heavy loads and bowed. Zopa responded by pulling his begging bowl out of his robe. The men quickly filled the bowl with rice and dried fish. Zopa gave them a blessing, and the men left with smiles on their faces.

"We have food," Alessia said.

"Yes," Zopa agreed. "But giving me food and receiving my blessing gave them confidence and a feeling of good luck, which is worth more than a few grains of rice and dried fish."

I wondered if the people in New York dropping coins into my baseball hat felt the same way.

Zopa turned to Nick. "Dr. Freestone, thank you for looking after my friends."

While Nick and Alessia talked to Zopa, I grabbed my binoculars and climbed a tree to get a better look at Hkakabo Razi. The mountain was cloudless. Through my binoculars, it looked like I could reach out and grab a handful of snow from the peak. It would have been a perfect day for a summit attempt, but the things I could reach with my eyes were several days away from my feet. What we needed to do when we got there was to climb fast and hope we didn't get bogged down by bad weather and route mistakes like Hiro and his team.

I heard shouting from below. I climbed around to the south side of the tree. Major Thakin and three soldiers with pointed rifles had arrived. Nick and Alessia had their hands in the air. Zopa did not. He was eating his rice from the bowl while the major shouted. I scrambled down the tree.

"Where is the other one!" the major shouted at me as I walked up.

"Ethan? He's up ahead at the next bridge."

"Where is Lwin?"

"I have no idea. You said he was dead."

"He is not dead! The finger belongs to another murdered by Lwin."

Or murdered by Lwin's elephant, I thought. I told him

about the slingshot attacks and Ethan *maybe* seeing Lwin at camp.

"Why would Lwin follow you? Why would he throw rocks?"

"That's what Ethan is trying to find out."

Major Thakin was not as crisp and clean as he had been during our first encounter. He and his men looked pretty beat-up. Their fatigues were torn, their eyes were bloodshot, and their faces and hands were covered with insect bites and scratches.

"And your friend is at the next bridge?" the major asked, looking wearily down the trail to the north.

"Yes," I said.

Zopa finished his rice, wiped the bowl clean, and stowed it inside his robe.

"And who are you?" the major asked.

Instead of answering, Zopa pulled a large cloth wallet out of his robe and handed it to Major Thakin. What else did he have stowed inside his robe? It appeared to be a bottomless Buddhist crevasse. The major sorted through the papers, checking them carefully. I wouldn't have been surprised if they were bogus. He had gotten Sun-jo into Tibet with forged papers on our way to climb the north side of Everest.

"These do not say what you are doing here."

"Pilgrimage."

"To where?"

Zopa shrugged.

"What direction are you heading?"

Major Thakin was being more deferential to Zopa than he had been to us. Probably because Zopa is a Buddhist monk and nearly ninety percent of Burmans are practicing Buddhists.

"North."

The major pointed at us. "Do you know these people?"

"Yes."

"Where did you meet them?"

"Here."

"I mean before."

"Afghanistan."

"Dr. Freestone does not have an Afghanistan visa in his passport."

"That's because I have never been to Afghanistan," Nick said impatiently, putting his arms down. "Interrogating us is not getting you any closer to Lwin Mahn. I want to be on the other side of this valley and across the bridge before nightfall. You can talk to us while we walk."

It looked like the major was going to object, but instead he said something to his men, who started down the hill to the north. I put my pack on and started after them. I was worried about Ethan and eager to get to the mountain. Fifteen minutes down the trail, I heard Alessia calling me. I had just passed the soldiers, who didn't seem to care. One of them had even smiled at me as I squeezed by them on the narrow trail. I felt guilty for ditching Alessia, but if I stopped and waited for her, the soldiers would catch up to me. I compromised by slowing down, which worked. She was able to slip past the soldiers.

"You are in a rush?" she asked cheerfully.

"Sorry. I wanted to get moving. There have been too many delays."

"You saw the mountain from the tree."

I grinned. "Yeah. It looked close. But a nineteen-thousand-foot mountain always looks close from a distance. And I'm worried about Ethan."

"And Zopa?"

Perceptive, kind, cheerful Alessia. I kissed her on the cheek. Her skin was salty.

"I am worried about Zopa," I admitted. "I love the guy, and I'm happy to see him, but something is up. It's not a coincidence, and he's not on a pilgrimage. I wish he'd tell me why he's here."

"But he will not."

"Not yet, anyway."

"He is talking now."

I looked back. We were way ahead of the soldiers, and beyond them I couldn't see anyone.

"He is talking to Major Thakin. When I left them, they were laughing."

It was hard to picture the major laughing. "What were they saying?"

"Their Burmese was too fast for me. Did you know that Zopa spoke Burmese?"

I shook my head. I wouldn't have been surprised to hear that Zopa was fluent in Martian. I was tempted to wait for Zopa and the major so Alessia could eavesdrop again, but my concern for Ethan kept me speeding down the trail.

"What did you learn from Hiro's photos?" Alessia asked.

I explained as we walked down the steep trail. At the bottom we found a short footbridge. We filled our water bottles and talked about waiting for the others, but decided to push on. There were more switchbacks, but we were able to skip a few that had narrow shortcuts straight uphill. They were slick with mud and difficult to negotiate, but they saved us a lot of time. We topped the hill drenched in sweat and out of breath. A short walk downhill led us to the final suspension bridge, which was still intact, but there was no sign of Ethan.

"He would be on the other side, would he not?" Alessia said.

The bridge was the highest we had encountered, and twice as long as the bridge we had helped to repair. We started across, moving slowly to minimize the sway, Alessia in the lead. Halfway across, Alessia stopped to look down at the raging river. I kept my eyes on the far side of the bridge, expecting Ethan to appear and greet us with his crooked grin. But he didn't show, and I got one of those Zopa *feelings* that something wasn't right.

I told Alessia that we needed to hurry and squeezed past her.

"What is wrong?"

"I don't know. Maybe nothing."

I ignored the sway as I rushed up the slippery planks. Ten feet from the end, I heard a rhythmic thumping sound and knew exactly what it was. I'd heard the same sound from the men working in the forest on the downed bridge. I shrugged out of my pack as I ran toward the anchor trees fifty feet up the hill. I had to fight my way through the foliage to reach the massive trunks. Lwin, or someone, had been there hacking away at the ropes. But where was he now? And where was Ethan? One of the ropes was cut almost all the way through, but there were several anchor ropes. The bridge was in no danger of collapsing unless the ropes on the other side had already been cut. I started over to the second tree, then stopped. If it was Lwin who had cut the rope, and I had little doubt it was, he was probably targeting me with his slingshot.

Or Alessia.

I ran back the way I had come.

Alessia was standing near the bridge. Her backpack was on the ground at her feet near my pack. Lwin was behind her, gripping her left arm. With his right hand, he was holding his *panga* to her neck.

EIGHTEEN

"DO NOT COME CLOSER, PEAK," Alessia said, pretty calmly considering that she had a maniac holding a knife to her throat.

I was standing thirty feet away from them, and I was anything but calm. I thought my heart was going to burst out of my chest. This was all my fault. I shouldn't have taken the shortcuts. I should have stuck close to the soldiers. They wouldn't arrive for at least an hour. Maybe longer. I took a couple of deep breaths, trying to slow my heart. It didn't work.

Lwin said something into Alessia's ear.

"He wants you to cut the bridge down," she said.

This was the time for Ethan to show up and save the day like he had done in the Pamirs. He was good at this. But if he was nearby, why hadn't he stopped Lwin when he started to slice the rope?

"I'll need his knife," I said.

Alessia actually smiled. A little. "I do not think he will give it to you."

"Are you okay?"

"Yes."

"Do you think he will really hurt you?"

"He might try."

"I'll have to cut the bridge."

Lwin shouted something and pushed the knife closer to her throat.

"He does not like our talking."

"Tell him that I need to get my hatchet out of my pack."

Alessia translated. Lwin backed away from the packs, the knife still at her throat. I walked slowly over, bent down, and unzipped a side pocket. As I pulled the hatchet out, I glanced at Lwin's tattered *longyi*. It was no longer bright and gaudy, but the worst thing was his feet. He was wearing Ethan's boots.

I stood up, shaken. "Did you see that he's wear—"

"Yes," Alessia said. "Ethan's hiking boots. I am . . . going to—"

Lwin started shouting again. I'm not sure what happened next, because it happened so fast. Lwin came flying over the top of Alessia's head. There was a loud snap, like a dry stick being broken, and then an unconscious Lwin was lying on the ground and Alessia was holding his *panga* to his neck. His nose and lip were bleeding. His two orange betel-nut-stained front teeth were missing.

"We will need something to tie him," Alessia said calmly.

I pulled some cord out of my pack. We tied his hands behind his back and bound his legs.

"How did you do that?"

"Ethan taught me." She pulled Ethan's boots off Lwin's

dirty feet. "I would have done it sooner, but we were standing too close to the edge. I did not want him to fall, or pull me over the edge with him. Before you came out of the forest, he told me that he was going to take me away with him."

I looked down at Lwin. His hand was twisted at an unnatural angle.

"I broke his hand. And probably his foot as well."

There was a purple bruise on his foot, but it was hard to see through the grime.

"We must find Ethan."

We tied Lwin to a tree, then split up and started searching. Ethan was either badly injured or dead. There was no other way Lwin could have gotten his boots. It must have happened just before we got there, otherwise Lwin would have already had the bridge down. How had Lwin gotten the drop on someone like Ethan? I stuck close to the anchor trees, thinking that Ethan would not have risked getting too far away from them. I called out his name over and over again and heard Alessia shouting his name in the distance. An hour passed. I was sick with dread.

"Hey."

I froze.

"Over here."

I followed the sound. Ethan was lying on the ground near a tree. If he hadn't said something, I would have walked right by. I might have even stepped on him. He blended in perfectly with the ground he was lying on.

He sat up and vomited. "Wow. Nasty. I must have fallen and hit my head on a tree."

"Maybe you should lie back down."

"Maybe I should."

I'd taken first aid for years. Something Mom had insisted on. Ethan had a concussion, and he had not fallen. There was dried blood on the side of his head and a lump the size of a chicken egg. He hadn't hit his head on a tree. Lwin had hit him with a projectile. I held his head and laid him back down.

"Just rest for a while. Take it easy."

I called out for Alessia.

"Alessia's here?" Ethan asked.

"Yeah."

"She shouldn't be out here alone. Lwin is around here somewhere."

"I know." I told him what Alessia had done.

"I told you she could kick your ass. It's weird. I feel like my feet are bare."

"That's because they are."

"I'm going to sit up."

"Not yet." I put my hand on his chest. "Lwin got you with his slingshot. He took your boots."

"No way."

"Yep. Just lie still."

He closed his eyes and appeared to drift off. Alessia came up behind me.

"He is alive?"

"Yes. But I don't like his looks. He's cold, and what skin I can see through the greasepaint is pale. He might be in shock. You stay with him. I'm going to get my first aid kit and an emergency blanket. Don't let him sit up."

I ran back to the bridge. The soldiers had arrived and were standing around Lwin, pointing their rifles at him. Zopa and the major were just stepping off the bridge.

I quickly explained what had happened as I rummaged through my pack for the first aid kit. The major peppered me with questions, which I ignored. I grabbed the kit, a pair of socks, and Ethan's boots, and ran back into the forest.

Ethan was struggling to sit up, but Alessia was having none of it. "Stop," she said firmly. "You must lie there like I have told you."

"It's just a bump on the head," Ethan protested. "Quit fussing over me. Jeez. Are those my boots?"

His boots were dangling around my neck. I handed them to Alessia. Ethan tried to sit up again.

"Not yet." I gently pushed him back down.

"I just need to put my boots on."

"And I need to clean up your head wound."

"I will put your boots on," Alessia said.

"I'm cold," Ethan said. "Dizzy. Yeah, put my boots . . ."

He passed out.

"Is it bad?" Alessia asked.

"I think so."

I put my headlamp on so I could see better. The bloody wound was covered with forest litter. I sluiced water over it. The nasty gash was an inch long, and deep. He was lucky to be alive. I disinfected my hands and picked the big pieces out with my fingers. Tweezers were next. When I finished, I poured more water over the wound, dried it with a sterile cloth, then looked at Alessia.

"This next part is going to wake him up. You'll need to hold his shoulders and head down."

She put her knees on his shoulders and her hands on his forehead. I poured disinfectant over the wound.

Ethan's eyes snapped open. "Hey!"

"Stop fighting it," I said. "Don't be a baby. Do you want your head to rot off?"

Ethan bit his lower lip. I noticed that his right pupil was bigger than his left. A sure sign of a concussion. I dabbed the peroxide off.

"You need stitches, but that's way beyond my skill set. I'm going to use butterfly bandages, then wrap your head."

I started to apply the bandages.

"I think I pretty much screwed up," Ethan said, wincing.

"You finally figured that out, huh?"

"My head is killing me. It feels like it's going to explode, but that's not the worst of it. I'm hallucinating."

"Yeah?"

"Yeah. Right now I see Zopa standing behind you in his monk clothes."

I turned around. Zopa had walked up behind us without making a sound. As usual.

Alessia laughed. "No. He is really here."

"How did—"

Zopa stepped forward and put his finger to his lips. "Do not talk. You need to be calm." He examined Ethan's head wound, then looked at his eyes. "You must lie completely still. Just breathe." He stepped away.

I finished applying the bandages, then wrapped his head

to hold everything in place. Ethan had closed his eyes again and was either asleep or unconscious. I walked over to Zopa.

"What do you think?" I asked quietly.

"It is a bad injury. We need to get him to a hospital."

"But first we need to get him to the bridge, where he'll be more comfortable. I'll go talk to the major."

"Major Thakin is gone."

"What?"

"He and the soldiers took Lwin south."

"Already?"

I didn't know if I was happy or ticked off about this. The soldiers could have helped us carry Ethan to the bridge, or maybe farther, but then we'd have had to deal with Major Thakin, who I didn't want to spend any more time with than I had to.

"We will make a litter and take him to the bridge," Zopa said. "We will watch him closely tonight. Perhaps he will be better in the morning."

NINETEEN

ETHAN WAS NOT BETTER the following morning. He was worse. He kept drifting in and out of consciousness. When he was awake, he was confused and frightened. He had no idea where he was or who we were. Alessia and I didn't leave his side all night long.

Nick crawled into the tent at sunrise to see how Ethan was doing.

"I'm not a medical doctor," he said. "But I think he's suffering from severe brain trauma. We need to get him to Yangon. That's the closest hospital that can deal with this kind of injury. I think he'll die if we don't get him there soon."

"I'm calling Chin," I said.

I found Chin's card and grabbed Ethan's sat phone. There was no signal from our campsite. The only clear spot in the canopy was the center of the bridge. I hurried along the slippery dew-covered boards and held the phone up. It acquired a satellite immediately. I punched in the number. It rang and rang, then went to voicemail. Frustrated, I left a message and disconnected.

Now what? If I left the bridge, I'd lose the signal and Chin's callback. If he called back. There was no guarantee of that. He could be anywhere now. He might be out of the country. And who knew if he was sincere when he had made the offer. And where was he going to land? There was no open space here. We'd have to move Ethan to get to the helicopter. How far would that be? Would he survive the move?

Zopa was tending the fire. The porters were still asleep on the ground near the donkeys. Nick was sitting outside his tent, writing in one of his notebooks. Ethan was inside his tent with Alessia. I sat down and let my legs dangle over the edge of the bridge. It was like sitting on a giant swing. Climbing Hkakabo Razi was over now, but I didn't care. It was a ridiculous idea in the first place. What were we thinking? I smiled. We were thinking like climbers. Optimistically. How else can you climb impossible things? Twenty minutes went by. Zopa took the rice off the coals and offered some to Nick, who joined him at the fire. Ten more minutes went by. Zopa disappeared into Ethan's yellow tent with a bowl of rice and a cup of tea. Five minutes later, he came back out. He waved and started toward the bridge. The sat phone rang.

"Peak?"

"Yes."

"What is the emergency?"

I told him.

"Where are you?"

I gave him our coordinates.

"One moment please."

Zopa started across the bridge.

"Peak?"

"Yes."

"I will call you back. I need to check with my pilot. Do not move from where you are. The signal is good."

Chin disconnected. I was relieved, even though he hadn't said that he was going to come, or when. Zopa was halfway to me. With his long robe, it looked like he was floating. For all I knew, he was floating. The bridge barely moved as he approached. Maybe he didn't even need a bridge. He sat down next to me.

"You talked with your friend?"

"Chin. Yeah. He's going to talk to his pilot and call back. How's Ethan?"

"No change."

"Is Chin the man's given name?"

"No. His name is Zhang Wei."

"Chinese."

"But he lives in Burma now." I explained how we had met him and his background.

"Ah, a climber," Zopa said. "They are everywhere."

I could no longer endure the mystery. "Why are you here, Zopa?"

"That remains to be discovered, but it is becoming clearer. I heard that you were climbing Hkakabo Razi."

"How did you hear that? I didn't know I was climbing Hkakabo Razi until I got to Burma."

Zopa laughed. "Your mother called me. I was in Tibet visiting monasteries not too distant from here."

Hundreds of miles, maybe a thousand miles, from here, I thought. Most of it on foot or in the back of dilapidated trucks, and this was not the only way to reach Hkakabo Razi.

He could easily have missed us in the rainforest. There was more to this than he was saying. With Zopa there was always more.

I glanced at Ethan's tent. "Well, we're not climbing the mountain now."

Zopa shrugged.

The phone rang.

"Peak?"

"I'm here."

"Good. Ethan is still with us?"

"Yes."

"We will pick Ethan up. There is a small logged-off area about six kilometers north of your current location. I will text you the exact coordinates after we finish this call."

"How soon will you be here?"

"Three, maybe four hours. I have spoken to a neurosurgeon in Yangon. His name is Vivek Deshmukh. He is the best. He will be calling you soon to ask about Ethan's symptoms and make some suggestions about how to transport him. He speaks Hindi, Burmese, and French. I would suggest you have Alessia speak with him."

"Okay. We have someone else here who could translate."

"Very good. I will come with just the pilot. The helicopter is very small. There will be room for Ethan to lie down with only one other person in back, and they cannot bring any equipment."

"No problem," I said. The other person would be Alessia. I walked here. I could walk back. But I would be lying if I said I was looking forward to it. I'd have to figure out a way to get their gear back to them. Nick could probably help me with that.

"I will have Dr. Deshmukh call in ten minutes."

"Thank you so much! I can't tell you how much I appreciate this."

"I hope I am in time."

He disconnected.

"Now you must go out and do good things," I said quietly.

"What is that?" Zopa asked.

"It's just a saying. Chin is flying in to pick up Ethan. He'll be here in three or four hours. We need to move Ethan six kilometers to the north. He said there is a clear-cut where the helicopter can land."

"I know the place," Zopa said.

I switched with Alessia, watching Ethan while she stood on the bridge awaiting Dr. Deshmukh's call. Alessia had removed the camo paint from Ethan's face. He had looked better with the camo. His face was bloodless, his pulse weak, and his head was swollen. Zopa and Nick were outside redesigning the crude litter we had put together the day before. I opened all the flaps and fanned Ethan with a map to keep him cool and the insects away. I talked to him on the off chance that he could hear from wherever he was. I told him about Zopa appearing out of nowhere. Chin coming to pick him up. Alessia's takedown of Lwin—

"He is conscious?" Alessia asked, putting her head in.

"No. I'm just talking to him. Letting him know that I'm here."

"I have been doing the same. You told him about Lwin?"

"Of course. I think that's one thing he would have liked to have seen for himself. What did Dr. Deshmukh say?"

"That we need to keep him as still as we possibly can when we move him. He said that we should strap him to the stretcher. Keep him level. Stabilize his head."

Luckily we didn't have any more switchbacks or giant hills in front of us, except for the mountain of course. If the map was right, there was a plateau a couple miles to the north leading up to Hkakabo Razi. I told Alessia that I thought she should accompany Ethan back to Yangon.

"This is my climb," she said. "And my fault. If I hadn't talked Ethan into—"

I put my hand on her shoulder. "Stop. You didn't talk Ethan or me into this climb. We were eager to go, eager to put the Pamirs behind us. Remember?"

She started to cry. I put my arms around her.

"You should fly back with Ethan," she said between sobs.

I held her at arm's length and wiped her tears. "With your connection to the embassy, you'll be able to get him better care than I could."

She gave me a reluctant nod. "Perhaps Chin can fly back and pick you up."

"I'll be fine. I'll have Zopa with me. At least I think he'll be with me. I haven't talked to him about it yet. I really don't like to ask Chin for another favor. He's done enough. Yangon is a long way from here. It's costing him a small fortune, to say nothing about his time."

"I do not think he would mind."

"We'll see what happens. I can stay in touch with you on the sat phone if the battery doesn't go dead."

"We will ask Chin for fresh batteries."

Nick stuck his head inside the tent. "I think we've cobbled together a decent litter. We should probably go."

THE LITTER WAS FINE, but it was nearly impossible to keep it level as we carried Ethan up the gentle grade. There were seven of us, including the porters. One of the porters had stayed back at the bridge to guard our gear and keep an eye on the donkeys. We took turns, stopping often to switch off and give our arms a rest. Ethan did not regain consciousness. We checked his pulse every time we stopped. It was weak, very weak.

It took us a little over three hours to get to the clear-cut. Ethan's condition was unchanged. We laid him in the shade of a tree, and Alessia wet a towel and wiped his face down in an attempt to cool him.

"I'll get more water."

Zopa and I walked across the clearing to a small stream. I took a drink. It was ice cold.

"Glacial," I said.

"Hkakabo Razi is not far from here," Zopa said. "A day's walk to the base." He started filling our spare bottles.

I had seen several of these clear-cuts during our trek, but all of them had been next to villages where they had used the wood for fuel and to build houses.

"There was no village here, so why did they cut the trees?" I asked.

"There used to be a village here," Zopa said, pointing to the western edge of the clearing. "A long time ago. People move on. The forest takes the land back."

I didn't see any sign of a village, but there was no other explanation for the clear-cut.

"Have you been here before?"

"Yes, on my way to find you."

We carried the water back to Alessia and waited. An hour passed, then another. Ethan was still breathing, but he looked like a corpse. If Chin didn't arrive soon, it would be too dark to land. I didn't know anything about brain injuries, but it didn't look like Ethan would make it through the night. I called Chin. It went to voicemail.

"I'm not sure how well sat phones work in a helicopter," Nick said. "It's hard to acquire a satellite while you're moving. I suspect he's on his way and will be here soon. I'm going to send the porters back to the bridge."

There was no point in his men sitting around and swatting bugs with us. The porters picked up what little they had brought with them and headed south.

Another hour passed. I started pacing like Ethan would have done if it had been me lying there dying. Zopa had found a shady spot at the edge of the clearing. He had been sitting for two hours and hadn't moved. I figured he was meditating, or maybe praying, or maybe both. He hadn't raised a hand to swat insects, and I was sure there were hundreds of them feeding on him.

I started to call Chin again, but my number punching was interrupted by the unmistakable sound of an approaching helicopter.

"Thank God," Alessia said.

"Amen to that." I looked over to Zopa. He hadn't moved. The helicopter circled the clearing a couple of times, sending every bird and monkey within miles fleeing for their lives. The third time around, the pilot feathered the helicopter in for a perfect landing fifty feet away from us. Chin was out of the cockpit and moving toward us before the rotors stopped.

"How is he?" He looked down at Ethan. "Not so well I see. I am sorry I am so late. We had to set up our refueling back to Yangon so we didn't have delays. We also removed the back seats from the helicopter so he would be more comfortable on the flight, and brought a real stretcher for him."

The pilot was pulling the stretcher out of the helicopter. Nick jogged over to give him a hand.

"Who is going with him?" Chin asked.

"Alessia," I said.

"Good. What about you?"

"I'll walk back. No big—"

"I will be with him, Zhang Wei." Zopa had walked up behind us.

Chin turned around and stared at Zopa in shock.

"I didn't mean to startle you," Zopa said.

Chin bowed. "You are he."

Zopa returned the bow. I had no idea what they were talking about.

"I am glad you survived. When I left you, I wasn't so sure. I hear that you took my advice."

"Now you must go out and do good things," Chin said with another bow.

PART

THREE

Hkakabo Razi

TWENTY

IT WAS A HASTY DEPARTURE. We transferred Ethan to the new stretcher, carried him carefully across the clear-cut, then slipped him into the helicopter. There was no time for Chin and Zopa to talk about their miraculous reunion, and barely time for me to say goodbye to Alessia. A hurried kiss. A worried look. Chin gave me a spare battery for the sat phone. And they were off.

"Damn!" I shouted.

"What?" Nick asked.

I pulled Ethan's spoon out of my pocket. "I meant to give this to Ethan before he took off."

"That's the least of his problems at this point," Nick said. "You can give it to him when you see him. I better check on the porters. You coming?"

"I'll be along soon." Everything had happened so quickly that I needed a few moments to wrap my mind around it. I sat down on one of the stumps in the clearing. Zopa took a seat on the stump next to mine. To the north I could just see the tip of a mountain peak, which one I didn't know, realizing that this was the closest I was going to get Hkakabo Razi.

Zopa pointed at the peak. "Hkakabo Razi."

"You've climbed it?"

"Not to the summit. I had to bring Zhang Wei down. This is where the village was. I am not certain he realized that when he landed here. He looks very much the same as he did back then."

"You must look the same too. He recognized you immediately. What are the chances of you meeting him out here in the exact same place you carried him?"

"I saved him. He saved Ethan. Karma."

The mystery, I thought.

"We don't know if Ethan will survive."

"I think he will. Negative energy is more easily kindled than positive energy. Best not to throw it in Ethan's direction."

"I'll try." And I would try. I'd do anything to save Ethan.

"Shall we go?"

I got up and decided that being with Zopa was a pretty good substitute for climbing Hkakabo Razi. I had been with him in two countries on two mountains, but I couldn't say that I knew him well. And I certainly didn't understand him. I suspected that nobody really knew him. And that was the way he liked it. He didn't say a word to me on the way back to camp. We arrived just before dark. Nick and the porters had food cooking, which I had smelled from a quarter mile away. We had neglected to bring anything to eat to the clear-cut, and I was famished.

"I'm heading out early tomorrow morning," Nick said,

as I wolfed the food down. I'm not even sure what it was. Some kind of stew and rice with globs of savory mystery meat. "My time's just about up. There are a couple more places I need to look at before I head back to Yangon. They're a little off the beaten path."

"I think everything is off the beaten path out here," I said.

"That's a fair point. What I mean is that it'll take me at least a couple weeks longer than you to get to Yangon. And I'm sure you're eager to check on Ethan."

I was eager to get back to Yangon. Chin had said there was a possibility that he could pick me up in his helicopter in six or seven days, which would save me a lot of wear and tear, and time.

"I do need to get back and check on him," I said.

"You can check on him with your phone," Zopa said.

"True, but that's not the same thing. And I only have one spare battery. We used three-quarters of the battery talking to Chin."

"You are under no obligation to go with me," Nick said. "I was fine when I ran into you, and I'll be fine without you, aside from missing your company. The porters will be disappointed, though. They are going to have to start climbing trees again. This has almost been a vacation for them."

"We are heading north," Zopa said.

"What?" I didn't think I had heard him correctly.

"North. Hkakabo Razi."

"I can't climb the mountain alone."

"I will go with you."

"I need to get back to Yangon."

"Ethan and Alessia would want you to climb."

"You're not dressed for an alpine climb."

Actually, he was barely dressed for a jungle walk. I looked at his feet. He was wearing sandals.

"I have the correct gear."

"Where?" There was no way he could have the appropriate gear concealed beneath his robe.

"At the base of the mountain. I left it there. No need to carry it through the jungle."

You never know what Zopa's real motivation is for doing something, Josh had said. *He's cagey.*

"You came here to climb?" I asked.

"It's what I do."

"I thought it was what you *did*. You told me you were retiring."

Zopa shrugged.

EARLY THE NEXT MORNING, Nick headed south with his porters and donkeys. Zopa and I headed north. I wasn't sure I wanted to climb Hkakabo Razi anymore. I'd given up on it when Ethan got hit. I checked the sat phone as we crossed the clear-cut. There had been no calls, which was good news. Alessia or Chin would have called if Ethan had died. My pack was heavy, overloaded with gear I had borrowed from Ethan and Alessia's packs before giving them to Nick to haul back to Yangon. I had almost taken Alessia's copy of *Stranger in a Strange Land*, but swollen like it was, it would have taken up too much room. The book must have weighed a couple of pounds, or two days' worth of freeze-dried food. Zopa had helped me with my load by carrying two heavy coils of rope bandolier style, crisscrossed over his saffron robe. He told me before we left that I was to lead the climb to the summit of Hkakabo Razi. It was nice of him to offer this, and I was flattered, but I doubted that it was going to happen. He was fifty yards ahead of me, moving at a good clip, his robe skimming the ground as if he were flying across the uneven trail toward the mountain.

We dipped down into what Zopa said was the last of the tangle. It was primeval. We started down at noon. Thirty feet in, I had to put my headlamp on in order to see. The only light came from tiny pinpricks of sun filtering through the canopy like dim stars. I offered my spare headlamp to Zopa. He said he didn't need it, but I noticed that he stopped ranging so far ahead. Swatting at the swarming insects was futile. We moved as fast as we could down to the dark valley floor, then up a long, steep trail with no switchbacks to ease the climb. I was mouth breathing by the time we reached the top. I had no idea how many insects I had inhaled when we finally broke out into sunshine. I squinted at the bright unfiltered light, swigged water, and spit the bugs out of my mouth. I shivered as cool air dried my sweat. It was like I had stepped from the inside of an active volcano into a refrigerator.

"Hkakabo Razi," Zopa said.

Before us was a broad alpine plateau of boulders, shrubs, small clusters of short trees, and snowfields. I took a deep breath of cool air, but I didn't have time to savor it because the sat phone rang. I answered with dread.

"Peak?"

It was Alessia.

"How's Ethan?"

"He is conscious."

My knees nearly buckled with relief.

"We are at the hospital in Yangon. Dr. Deshmukh has run a CT scan on him, and he says that the injury is serious, but he is hopeful. They are doing more tests right now."

"How was Ethan when he came to . . . when he regained consciousness?"

"Agitated. It was difficult to keep him still in the back of the helicopter."

I could imagine.

"He did not know where he was. He did not know what had happened to him. It took him some time to recognize who I was. When we arrived at the hospital, they gave him something to settle him down."

"How are you?" I asked.

"Very tired. I am going to get some sleep in the waiting room, but I wanted to call you first. I miss you."

"I miss you too."

"Chin says that he will be able to pick you up in a week, or perhaps ten days' time, depending on where you are."

I looked at the snowfields up ahead. "Do you need me back there right away?"

"I would of course like to see you, but no. And how would you get here right away? I think Ethan is in good hands. I feel optimistic. But Dr. Deshmukh thinks that Ethan will be here for a minimum of two weeks."

I could be at the summit and back in a week to ten days.

Chin could pick me up right where I was. Plenty of places to land.

"I'm at the base of Hkakabo Razi," I said.

There was a long silence. I looked at the phone's screen, thinking that I had lost the connection, then Alessia said, *"You traveled north instead of south?"*

"With Zopa."

"Are you going to climb to the summit?"

"We're going to try."

I remember what Zopa told me on Everest. *You can never tell who the mountain will allow and who it will not.*

"It won't be the same without you and Ethan."

"No. But I am glad that you are going to try. At least one of us might reach the summit. If not, what have all of the hardships been for?"

"True."

"Do you think this is why Zopa came to Burma?"

"He told me that's why he came. My mom told him we were trying for the mountain. This doesn't explain how he found us in the middle of nowhere, because she didn't know where we were. When you get a chance, tell my mom that I'm with him."

"You will stay in touch with me?"

"Of course. And can you tell Chin that he might be picking me up at the base of the mountain when we're finished?"

"He has already left Yangon on business. But I will tell him. He was very excited to see Zopa."

Don't ask me how, but I think Zopa knew he was going to run into Chin. I didn't mention this to Alessia because I didn't want to burn up what battery I had left.

"I'm going to keep this phone turned off to preserve the battery. I think it has voicemail. If I don't answer, leave me a message."

Alessia laughed. *"Yes, if you even remember that you have a phone in your pack."*

She knew me well.

TWENTY-ONE

ZOPA KEPT WALKING. His gear was not hidden away in the first or second stand of trees, or behind one of the many boulders scattered up the slope. When I asked him where his gear was stowed he'd say, "Up ahead. Not far."

Not far led us across a three-mile-long ice field blanketed with crackly snow six inches deep. I scooped some into my water bottle. It was so cold it made my teeth ache.

Not far took us along the base of a glacial cliff. I stopped and put on a fleece that in the jungle I'd thought I would never come to use. I asked Zopa how his feet were. He was still wearing sandals.

"Cold, but they are fine. Do you have a spare headlamp?"

I looked up at the sky. It was late afternoon. We had hours of light left. "We're going to need headlamps?"

"Yes."

"Where's your gear?" I asked again.

"Not far."

I gave him my spare headlamp. We walked on. I wondered if Zopa was lost. I wondered if he had gotten senile. I didn't know how old he was, but he was getting up there. Perhaps his mind had slipped. Perhaps he thought he was on Everest, or back on one of the other countless mountains he had climbed. It began to snow. Tiny ice pellets at first, then larger flakes big enough to catch with the tip of my tongue. I stopped to put on a sock cap and a down vest. When I caught back up with Zopa, I offered him my spare cap and vest. He took them without a word.

"I'm getting a little nervous," I said.

"No need." He snugged the cap over his ears and re-bandoliered the ropes over the vest.

"I'm worried about your feet."

"No need." He lifted the hem of his robe. He was wearing heavy hiking boots with thick socks.

"Where did you get those?"

"I had them strung around my neck beneath my robe. It is a relief to have them on my feet. The laces were chafing my neck. Did you think I would climb a mountain in sandals?"

"I didn't see you put the boots on."

Zopa shrugged, then forged ahead.

The sun went down. The temperature dropped. The snowfall got heavier. I couldn't see twenty feet in front of me. Our headlamps glittered against the snowflakes. I turned on my GPS watch. I had kept it off to conserve the battery. It took a while to acquire a satellite signal, and I was shocked when the elevation popped up. We were at a little over 9,000 feet. How had that happened so quickly? I turned on the sat phone to see if Alessia had left a message about Ethan. She hadn't.

Zopa stopped at 9,500 feet and waited for me to catch up. "How is your head?" he asked.

"I have a headache. We've gained a lot of altitude."

Zopa took in a deep breath. "Ten thousand feet?"

"Are you wearing an altimeter watch?"

He shook his head and smiled. "I am an altimeter. Three thousand feet to go. But we can stop here and camp if you like."

I was tired and out of breath from the sudden altitude gain, but I wanted to get where we were going, or where Zopa was going.

"Let's push on."

And we did. I glanced at my watch every few minutes to check the altitude, wishing I had turned in on when we left the jungle so I knew how far we had climbed. At 10,000 feet, my head started to really pound. I didn't think I was getting high altitude sickness, but the headache was a clear sign that I had climbed too high too fast. I tried to keep myself hydrated because I knew that would help. At 11,000 feet, we started up a steep slope. *Climb high, sleep low,* was the mantra on Everest. If my headache got worse, I might have to follow this advice.

We trudged upward. The snowfall lessened, but the wind picked up—a steady twenty miles an hour with gusts to fifty that nearly blew me over backward. I leaned forward, trying to keep a low profile, which did not help my headache. Every hundred steps, I had to stop and put my hands on my knees to catch my breath. When I was two hundred feet behind him, Zopa finally glanced back and stopped long enough for me to catch up.

"You okay?" Unlike me, Zopa was not mouth breathing. He looked like he could climb right to the summit.

"Out of breath," I gasped.

"It will be better in the morning. Not far."

I had stopped believing in *not far*.

When we reached 12,000 feet, I was pretty much done. I wanted to slide back down to the place Zopa had suggested we camp. I was depleted. I hadn't eaten enough, and even though I had forced myself to drink, I was dehydrated. In my defense, I hadn't known that we were actually going to start the climb as soon as we popped out of the blistering tangle.

At 12,500 feet, I was on the verge of collapse. I needed to turn back, spend a day at a lower elevation and try again. The problem was that I couldn't turn back without telling Zopa, who was fifty or sixty feet in front of me, steadily moving up a steep rise. I shouted, but his name was blown off the mountainside by the howling wind. If I turned back in this weather without him knowing, we might not ever find each other. I stared ahead at his bouncing headlight, willing myself to catch it like the fireflies I had chased when I was a kid. The game started to work. His beam became bigger and brighter as I gained on him. I was going to catch the firefly! And I did . . . Because Zopa was standing perfectly still at the top of the rise, and no doubt had been doing so since I started the game. I put my hands on my knees and tried to suck in enough O's to speak.

"I think . . ." Gasp . . . "I need to . . ." Gasp . . . "Go back . . ." Gasp . . . "Down . . ." Gasp . . . "Climb high . . ." Gasp . . . "Sleep . . ." Gasp . . . "Low."

"Good idea," Zopa said. "But I think it would be wiser to go forward." He pointed. At the bottom of the rise, thirty feet away, were six tents. Two yellow, two red, one blue, one green, lit up like Christmas decorations in the snow. The green tent was four times bigger than the other tents.

"Who—"

"Let's walk down and see," Zopa said.

I stumbled down behind Zopa in a daze, thinking the lit tents were some kind of mountain mirage. The camp was sheltered from the harsh wind. I could hear our footsteps breaking through the crisp snow. Zopa opened the flap of the green tent. I stared in disbelief. Yogi and Yash were sitting across from each other playing cards at a portable camp table. The Nepalese brothers, good friends of Zopa's, had led Sun-jo and me on our final ascent to the summit of Everest. They jumped up from the table and greeted us with bows and broad grins. I was still out of breath, but the warmer air inside the tent was easing the distress. They clapped me on the shoulder and began chattering in Nepalese. I dropped my pack and began to feel as if I might survive. Yogi brought me a mug of steaming hot soup, which I felt all the way down to my toenails.

"What are you doing here?" I asked, grateful to have my voice back without gasping.

"Climbing Hkakabo Razi with you," Yash answered with a crooked-tooth smile.

Yogi refilled my mug.

"How long have you been here?"

"Five days," Yash said.

"No," Yogi said, holding up six fingers.

"Did you see the Japanese climbers?"

The brothers didn't understand the question and looked at Zopa. He translated and they shook their heads.

"Big mountain," Yash said. "Easy to not see them."

I looked at Zopa. "So you planned this all out."

"A surprise. A gift for what you did for Sun-jo on Everest. And for what Ethan did for us in the Pamirs."

This sounded to me like Zopa was being cagey again. I think what happened is that he thought Hkakabo Razi was too big for us, too tough. And he was probably right.

"I'm glad," I said. "Thank you." I smiled at Yogi and Yash. "Thank you all."

I pulled the sat phone out of my pack. I turned it on. There was a voice message from Alessia.

"Peak . . . There is little change in Ethan's condition. They are keeping him sedated in the intensive care unit so that he does not move. There is some swelling in his brain that they are worried about. They may have to operate, but have not yet decided. They have put a drain into his skull to lessen the swelling. I am at the hospital still, but I am returning to the embassy to change my clothes, and perhaps sleep. I spoke to my mother. She is returning to Yangon tomorrow because she is concerned about Ethan. You have probably not heard, but your father completed his climb in record time six days ago. There was an interview with him on the television. He looked tired, but happy. He said he was going to return to his home and sleep for two weeks. I do hope to meet him one day soon and that Ethan recovers so he can meet him too. I left a message for your mother saying that you are with Zopa and safe. I will call you again tomorrow after I check on Ethan. Please be safe on the mountain when you begin your climb. I miss you."

Alessia didn't know I had already started the climb and that I was at 13,000 feet, sipping soup, trying to breathe. I put the phone on speaker and replayed the message for Zopa. Yash and Yogi listened as well. They understood English better than they spoke it.

"Can I stay in here tonight?" I asked. I didn't have the energy to prepare a campsite and set up my tent.

"This is your climb," Zopa said. "Your camp. You may sleep wherever you wish."

This had ceased to be my climb the moment Zopa showed up, but at that moment I didn't care. All I wanted to do was sleep. I pulled out my sleeping bag and pad. As I was rolling them out, the tent flap opened, letting in freezing cold air and my dad, Joshua Wood.

TWENTY-TWO

WHEN I WOKE UP THE NEXT MORNING, it took me a couple seconds to remember where I was. My shortness of breath reminded me that I was at 13,000 feet on Hkakabo Razi. I lay there watching the sun filter through the green tent fabric, thinking about the night before.

Josh had summited Everest eight days ago. When he got back down to the Nepal base camp, he conducted a dozen media interviews, then told everyone that he was returning to his home in Chiang Mai to recuperate. *"World's best climber will reconnect with the world after well-deserved rest."* The quote and adjoining article had gone viral on social media. But Josh had no intention of going home, or resting.

Sometimes the best thing to do after a triumph is to disappear, he had told me.

I wondered if he had learned this from Zopa, who was always disappearing and reappearing when you least expected.

"When Zopa said you were going to try for Hkakabo Razi," Josh continued, "I told him that I was in—if I wasn't too hammered after the seven summits. I'll admit that I was

a little wrecked after Everest, but I'm fine now. I haven't
done anything since I got here four days ago except to eat
and sleep. We expected you a couple days ago. Where's your
team?"

I told him what had happened to my *team*.

"Wow! Crazy elephant driver. What do you think the military did with him?"

I shrugged. Lwin had tried to kill Ethan. I'd know in the
next few days if he had succeeded. I didn't care what happened to the crazy mahout.

I was happy that Josh had shattered the world's record.
This would certainly help Peak Experience, which I should
point out was not named after me. High-paying clients would
be lined up outside his tent for a chance to climb with the famous Joshua Wood. But why was he here? There was no glory
in climbing Hkakabo Razi except to find out how tall it was.
This wasn't Josh's thing. I suspected that Josh was being just
as cagey as Zopa, but unlike Zopa, if you asked Josh a direct question, he'd answer it, even if it wasn't the answer you
wanted to hear.

"I still don't get it," I said. "Why are you here?"

"Several reasons. You and I have never climbed together.
I mean, we were on Everest together, and you were on my
permit, but you climbed with Zopa, Yogi, and Yash."

"And Sun-jo," I added.

Josh nodded. "I hear he's getting a lot of endorsement
deals. That could have been you."

*Oh boy, the same old conversation Ethan had with me in
Yangon.* "I'm glad it isn't me," I said.

Josh smiled. "I keep forgetting. You have my DNA, but

we're wired a little differently. You're more like your mom. I've always wondered what she would have been like if she hadn't had that accident when you were a baby."

She wouldn't have a limp, I thought. She might not have met Rolf and had the twins, whom I adore. The fall had done more for her and Rolf and me than we'll ever know.

"She climbed well in the Pamirs," I said, which was an exaggeration. None of us had gotten much of a chance to climb in the Pamirs. I had written to Josh about what had happened to us in Afghanistan, but I didn't know if he had read the letter or not. He hadn't written back. His letters, emails, or even texts were as rare as weather openings on Everest. This didn't bother me much anymore. I didn't expect him to respond. I would have been surprised if he had.

"It sounded pretty dicey in the Pamirs. I was glad to hear you were all right . . . and your mom of course."

"Of course," I said, trying not to sound too snide. "What are the other reasons you're here?"

"Zopa," he answered. "His son saved me up on K2 and died because of it. That's a debt that can never be repaid. Zopa asked me to make this climb with you."

"Did he say why?"

"No. When I asked, he shrugged."

We both laughed at this. A shrug was Zopa's answer for everything he didn't want to answer.

"The final reason is kind of selfish," Josh said. "Or selfserving, anyway. I've made a splash with my latest climb, but I've learned that the ripples get weaker the farther they travel from the initial impact. I know I wasn't forthcoming with you on Everest. I mean . . ." He hesitated. "I did help you out of that skyscraper jam in New York, but . . ." Another hesitation. "Do you remember when you confronted me at base camp?"

I remembered every word of the confrontation and didn't regret one word that I had said.

"You called me out," Josh said. "And rightly so. I was using you and your age to help my business. It might have helped you too if you had gotten to the summit."

"But not as much as it has helped Sun-jo," I said. "He and his sisters have a future now. They can go to school. They can become anything they want to become."

"Is that why you decided not to summit? Yogi and Yash told me that you were less than twenty steps away."

I shrugged, not to be mysterious or obtuse, but because I still didn't know the answer, and I was getting comfortable with not knowing.

"Okay," Josh said. "I'm sure you had your reasons. Back to those ripples and me being straight up with you. I could do a hundred more interviews next week, but if I did, everyone would be sick to death of me by the end of the following week. The only way for me to keep the seven-peak momentum going is to put it behind me and keep climbing. Hkakabo Razi is the perfect mountain for this, and you are the perfect partner for the climb."

I could just see the articles now:

JOSHUA WOOD CONQUERS HKAKABO
RAZI WITH HIS SON, PEAK

After smashing the world record on the seven summits,

Joshua Wood takes his son on the climb of his
life.

Blah . . . blah . . . blah . . .

It would have been nice if Josh had just wanted to climb
with me, but that was never going to happen. That's not who
Josh is. I didn't like him any less for it, and I didn't love him
any more for it either. At least this time he was barely using
me. In fact, he really didn't need me to accomplish his ripple
effect. Summiting Hkakabo Razi right after the seven summits would be impressive with or without me.

"Thanks for letting me know," I said.

"So you understand?"

"I get it," I answered.

"Good. That went better than I thought it would. The
truth can be awkward. JR and Will are back in the States deal-
ing with the hundreds of hours of video they and others shot
on the seven summits."

"Where's Jack?" I asked with a sinking feeling in the pit
of my stomach. Jack was the third member of JR's crew. I
thought I already knew the answer to where Jack was. There
were five other tents on the slope. Yash's, Yogi's, Zopa's, Josh's.
One extra tent, and it wasn't mine. A yellow tent. The same
color the crew used in the Pamirs.

"Funny you should ask," Josh said.

"Because he's here," I said.

"How'd you know?"

"A wild guess."

"He's going to film us," Josh said enthusiastically, like a

salesman trying to sell something nobody wanted. "What do you think?"

"I like Jack," I said, which was true. "But what do you mean by 'us'? We had in mind a clean climb without any documentation. In fact, we left our cell phones back in Yangon so we wouldn't be tempted."

"Old school, huh?"

I nodded.

"I guess I could have Jack wait for us here at base camp," Josh said.

I smiled at the weak, and absolutely insincere, offer. "I told you that I totally get what you're trying to do. Jack can film you. No problem, but I don't want him to film me. I don't want to be mentioned in any article or documentary. I didn't come here . . . *We* didn't come here for that. There will be no do-overs, or delays for the light to be right, or waiting for Jack to get ahead of us for continuity. He'll have to keep up and settle for what he can get in real time. I'm not here to be in a documentary, or to get attention, or to make money. I'm here to climb."

Josh's smile broadened. "I won't argue with you at this point. You're tired, and you're not acclimated. I'll talk to Zopa and see what he thinks. We'll revisit the topic in the morning."

NOW IT WAS MORNING, and pretty soon I would find out who was going to lead the climb.

Zopa, Josh, or me. I didn't think it was going to be me. Our simple climb had been co-opted, which wasn't uncommon in high-altitude climbs. I didn't blame Josh for trying to take it over. He was the obvious leader for any climb, but I did wonder how much research he had done for this climb. I suspected very little, because there wasn't much out there about Hkakabo Razi and he had been flat-out busy climbing the seven summits.

I was a little sore and limb-weary, and I still had a head-ache, but my breaths were coming easier, which was a relief. I got dressed, stepped outside, and squinted at the morning light reflecting off the snow. It was cold and foggy. Visibility about forty or fifty yards.

Jack was the first one out of his tent. He was bundled in a red snowsuit, a matching muffler, a red sock cap, and a camera bag slung over his shoulder. He waved. I waved back. I hadn't seen him since we went our separate ways in Afghanistan. We shook hands.

"Are you ready for this?" he asked. "Is there coffee inside? Where's Ethan and Alessia?"

I told him that they weren't climbing and explained why.

"Oh my God! A slingshot? Is Ethan going to be okay?"

"Don't know yet."

We went inside. I switched the sat phone on. No messages.

Next up were Yash and Yogi. They came into the green tent together, cheerful as always, and started the water boiling. Last in were Zopa and Josh. Zopa had changed into his climbing clothes. Josh was all smiles and energy.

"We're kind of socked in this morning, which is just as well," he announced to everyone. "Peak needs another day to acclimate and rest. We'll plan to move up to a higher camp first thing tomorrow morning, weather permitting. This will give us a chance to sort gear and repack today."

I guessed that Josh had talked to Zopa and they had agreed that he would be in charge of the climb. Big shock.

"Jack's going to be doing a little filming," Josh continued. He looked at me. "We'll make sure he doesn't slow us down too much. Jack knows the routine. We all know the routine. Jack is good, he'll—"

"This is not your climb," Zopa said quietly.

"What?" Josh asked as if he hadn't heard correctly, which was ridiculous, because we were in a tent that was barely big enough for six people.

"This is Ethan's climb and Alessia's," Zopa said. "Now that they have had to abort, this is Peak's climb. He is the leader unless he wants to pass the leadership on to someone else. The choice is his alone."

Alone was right. Five people in the tent with me, ten eyes staring at me, and I was totally alone. I guess Josh *hadn't* had time to talk to Zopa. Yogi and Yash were the first to look away from me. I don't think it mattered to them who led the climb. Their immediate problem was who was going to make breakfast. They cut cards to see who would cook. I hoped Yogi would win; Yash was a much better cook. Yash drew a two of clubs and swore. Zopa stepped over to the burner and poured boiling water into his mug. This left just two sets of eyes on me. Josh's and Jack's, although Jack wasn't staring, he was flipping between me and Josh, looking a little bewildered.

I was bewildered too. The obvious choice was to relinquish the climb to Josh, but this wasn't his climb. If I backed down, the intent of the climb would be completely changed. I thought about suggesting that we co-lead the climb, but rejected it, knowing that co-leading never worked. If Alessia and Ethan had been here, I wondered which way they would have gone. I chastised myself. There was no use speculating. The decision was up to me. And I had to make the decision right now because waiting too long was a sign of weakness.

"I'm going to lead the climb," I said with as much confidence as I could muster. "We'll sort and repack this morning. If the weather clears, we'll leave this afternoon for the next camp, fourteen thousand feet, give or take." We wouldn't know exactly where the camps would be until we got there.

Yash and Yogi nodded, as if this was perfectly fine. Zopa smiled. Josh was smiling too, but I wasn't sure how sincere it was. Jack looked worried. I didn't blame him. I was worried too.

"I know that Josh wants to film some of the climb," I continued, looking at Jack. "And that's okay, but I don't want to be in the film. That's not why I'm here. We aren't slowing down for anything. You'll have to keep up and take what shots you can get. The goal is to get to the top of Hkakabo Razi and get back down."

Jack glanced at Josh, then gave me a reluctant nod.

"I talked to the Japanese climbers. I made some sketches and took a lot of notes. I think we should all look them over now and figure out our best route."

Without waiting for an answer, I pulled my notebook out of my pack, and the long discussion began.

TWENTY-THREE

THE DISCUSSION TOOK THE BETTER PART of two hours. It was mostly a two-way conversation between me and Josh with four silent onlookers. It reminded me of the route debates Mom and I had when I was a kid, but this was more intense. On the outside, Josh appeared to have accepted me as the team leader, but I had a feeling that just below the surface, his feelings were very different. I can't say that I blamed him. Josh had been top dog on every mountain he had climbed for the past two decades. It was hard to say who was the tougher debater, Mom or Josh. We compared my notes and sketches to satellite maps and a crude drawing that Josh had of Takashi Ozaki's 1996 route up the north face to the summit. He was one of the only climbers to top Hkakabo Razi. We could have debated the route for days, but our discussion, or argument, was interrupted by bright sunlight shining through the green tent. The weather had cleared.

It took us less than two hours to break camp and redistribute the gear. Yash and Yogi were experts at this, maybe the best in the world. Zopa claimed that they did not spend a month under a roof in any given year. The only family they had was each other. They had spent nearly thirty years in the Himalayas hauling gear, cooking, and setting up camps for climbers and trekkers.

"You wouldn't know it to look at them, but the brothers are wealthy," Zopa commented as we watched them from a distance.

"Seriously?"

"They haven't had to spend a rupee of their own money in decades. They are fed and sheltered, and even clothed by the climbers and trekkers they serve."

"Did you pay them for this climb?"

Zopa shook his head. "They volunteered. For you."

Speaking of paying, Josh walked up to the brothers, spoke to them a moment, then started peeling off bills from a wad he had stashed in his pocket.

"What's he . . ." I started in his direction.

Zopa put a restraining hand on my shoulder. "Let it go. Pick your arguments. This is not one of them. Josh is paying them to carry some of Jack's load, which is not a bad idea. He is a good climber, but not a great climber, and he is not nearly as strong as Yash and Yogi. No one here is." Zopa smiled. "And they do like their money, even though they don't spend it. Look at them grin."

They were grinning.

"I don't want them slowed down by the extra weight."

"You are making a joke. Yogi and Yash are two-legged yaks. Let's talk about your route again. Get out your map."

"Is there a problem with it?"

"No. But I do not have it in my head like you do. Show me where you think the camps will be."

I spread out my rough route map on a boulder. By the time we finished looking it over, everyone was ready to go.

TO OUR RIGHT WAS the avalanche-tumbled glacier that Hiro and his team had discovered to be impassable. They had spent an entire day trying to get through it and another day retracing their steps back to base camp. Directly in front of us was a 2,000-foot spire. Hiro had said there was a shelf big enough for a few tents at 14,107 feet, or 4,300 meters. We walked up to the base and put our heads back. The top of the spire was shrouded in mist.

"Camp One, thirteen hundred feet up," I said to no one in particular.

The bad news was that there was steady twenty-five-mile-an-hour wind gusting to thirty or forty miles across the wall. The good news was that it was ten degrees below zero, which meant that our ice anchors would not pop out.

"Kind of blustery," Josh said, squinting against the bitter wind.

I shrugged out of my pack and started to strap crampons over my boots. "I'll climb first and set protection. The face looks pretty level. I think we can rope our packs up to camp."

"I agree," Josh said. "You want me to go first?"

I hadn't noticed before, but he had an action camera strapped to his helmet. Jack was standing next to Josh. He had an action camera too.

"Are those things on?"

Josh looked at Jack.

"They're rolling," Jack admitted. "I'm controlling both cameras with a remote. We'll edit out any vid of you. I can switch them off if you want."

"Don't bother." I looked at Josh. "I'll go first, but I appreciate the offer." And I did appreciate it. He wasn't trying to co-opt the climb by volunteering. He was being practical. He had a lot more experience climbing everything with the exception of skyscrapers. But the person leading the climb was not always the best climber. The reason I wanted to go first was because I didn't know if the shelf was there. It could have sloughed off in the past week, an avalanche could have destroyed it, and there was a chance, a small chance, that Hiro was talking about a different spire. Yogi and Yash hadn't seen the Japanese climbers, which meant that their base camp could have been miles from where the brothers had set up our base camp. If the camp wasn't at 14,107 feet, or if it wasn't usable, I'd be the only member of my team to waste energy on a dead end.

My team. This was the first time I had thought of the others this way, and the thought made me smile.

"What's so funny?" Josh asked.

"Nothing. I guess I'm just looking forward to climbing a wall. It's been a while."

"Are your O's okay?"

"I haven't even thought about them since I woke up this morning."

"Watch the wind," Zopa said, tying the belaying rope onto my harness.

I took one last look up the wall, visualizing the ascent, then slammed the steel toe tip into the ice and started up. The windswept cold was brutal, but I could not have been happier. I was alpine climbing. Left toe point in . . . pull up with right-handed ax . . . right toe point in . . . pull up with left-handed ax. Repeat. I placed my first ice screw at twenty feet, attached a carabiner, clipped the rope in, then continued up the wall one toe point at a time.

At 13,500 feet, the wind gusts got stronger. I hugged the wall so I didn't get peeled off. At 13,700, the mist dropped. I lost sight of my team below. I couldn't see three feet ahead. The lactic acid was building up in my arms and legs, and my lungs burned a little, but overall I felt pretty good. My biggest worry now was missing the ledge, if it existed, in the thick mist. A sheet of ice broke loose under my ax.

"Ice!" I shouted in warning, hanging on to the wall with only my left toe point and left ax. I slammed my right ax into the ice above. It didn't stick.

"Clear!" Josh shouted from below.

The rope tightened. Zopa was belaying me. He knew I was in trouble. I swung the ax again. It didn't stick. Again. In, but not solid enough. My left side started to tremble with fatigue. I had one more swing in me before I fell. I heaved upward and swung. The ax stuck. I pulled myself up and slammed in a toe point, which was enough to take the weight off my left side. Secure now, I pulled the left ax out of the wall and gave my rope three quick jerks. Zopa relaxed the belay and gave me some slack. I breathed a sigh of relief and tried to catch my breath. This whole problem had taken less than two minutes. This is how climbing works. Hours of muscle-burning work interrupted by heart-stopping panic. My smile had turned a little grim, but I was still smiling.

The next three hundred feet were pretty straightforward. The ice was solid. The wind died down. It started to snow. Visibility was nearly zero. It was like I was climbing through a dense cloud. At 14,000 feet, I slowed down. If I wasn't careful I could climb right past the ledge, if it was even there, which I was beginning to doubt. Josh had offered me a two-way radio before I started up. I passed, telling him that I would just give a yank on the rope when I reached the ledge. Now I wished I had taken the radio. I could have had Josh climb up and help me look. The ledge could have been fifty feet higher, fifty feet lower, to my right, or to my left. If I didn't find it soon, it would be too late for the others to make the ascent before dark. Then I caught a bit of color from the corner of my eye. I turned my head, and saw nothing but white. I waited. The mist shifted. I saw it again for a half second. It was green, twenty feet to my left. I traversed over to the spot. It was a green fuel canister. The Japanese climbers must have left it behind. Five feet above it was the ledge. It must have rolled off and caught. A little miracle, because I was certain the Japanese climbers were just like us: *When you break camp, it should look like you were never there.* If the canister hadn't rolled out of view, I might never have found the ledge. I hoisted myself up. It was fifteen feet wide, ten feet deep, and stable, with only a little ice debris that had to be cleared. I gave the rope three quick jerks. My signal was answered with one jerk. I started smoothing out the surface for our tents. Camp One.

TWENTY-FOUR

WE STARTED EARLY THE NEXT MORNING. We had a 2,500-foot climb to Camp Two with full packs, because much of the climb would be traverses. You can't rope a pack horizontally. Once again, Josh offered to take the lead, and this time I gladly consented, without acting too eager. I'd proved my point the day before by leading the way to Camp One. And truth be told, I was pretty wiped out, even after a good night's sleep.

Camp Two was a vague idea rather than an actual place. It would be an up-and-down climb starting with a traverse to the northeast, skirting a glacier, then a climb up the spire behind where we were camped, then down to another glacier where we would zigzag our way up another smaller spire. Our goal was to get to the ridge leading to the summit by the end of the following day. I'd decided to keep to the ridges as much as possible to stay above avalanche threat. We'd heard one let loose the night before somewhere to the west. It was misty, with a visibility of about fifty feet. More worrisome was the temperature. It was twenty-five degrees out, still cold, but thirty-five degrees warmer than the day before. If it warmed up any more, we could be in serious trouble from ice melt and avalanches.

"We need to beat the thaw," Josh said, taking off across the face, climbing about three times faster than I had climbed the day before. It was an amazing thing to watch.

I was to go next, followed by Zopa, Yash, and Yogi. Jack asked if he could stay back to take some drone shots of Josh traversing the face.

"Sure. But don't take too long. We need to . . ." I changed my mind. "I'll hang back with you. I don't want anyone climbing alone today." What I really meant by this was that I didn't want our weakest climber taking up the rear spot. "Do you have a radio?"

"Yeah."

"Better give it to me. I'll follow you across."

So, now I was carrying a radio and actively participating in Josh's video. What next? I clipped the radio to my harness and walked over to Zopa to explain the new order of things. He and the brothers started the traverse carrying packs almost as heavy as they were. My pack was none too light either. Jack started assembling the drone, happy that the wind had died down enough for him to use it. He fired it up and did a few experimental flights, then put on a pair of goggles.

"It's like I'm right in the cockpit. There's a tablet in my pack. You can follow along if you like."

What I wanted to do was get moving and get this over with. This is exactly what happens when you turn a climb into a film production. It becomes more about the shot than it does about the climb. I pulled the tablet out of his pack and turned it on.

Whoa! I thought. Despite my grumbling, I had to admit that the vid was pretty impressive. The drone caught up with Zopa and the brothers making their way across the wall on the fixed rope Josh had set. With the heavy packs on their backs, they looked like enormous turtles. They were in high definition, with every spray of ice from their axes crystal clear. Jack followed the rope up behind Josh. He was a hundred feet ahead of the others, setting an ice screw. He must have sensed the drone because he turned and gave it a thumbs-up and a charming smile. That's my dad.

"We better wrap this up," I said.

Jack retrieved the drone and packed it. I checked the temperature. Thirty degrees. I had Jack go first, telling him to hurry, but to be safe. I took up the rear, pulling out protection, making it look like we were never there. Somehow, focusing on the softening wall, removing the hardware, took my weariness away. Jack was a couple hundred feet in front of me, moving well. His climbing skills had obviously improved while he was filming Josh on the seven summits. Halfway across the face, I glanced at my watch. Thirty-three degrees. The surface of the ice was watery. Leaving the protection in place might have been the smartest thing to do, but I really didn't like leaving steel on the mountain. This had been drilled into me since I was a little kid. One of the things I hated about Everest was that people left almost everything behind. The six camps leading to the summit on the northern side looked like solid waste disposal sites.

The two-way crackled, startling me. I had forgotten I had it clipped to my harness.

"Peak?"

It was Josh. I had to rearrange my hold to free up a hand. "Yeah."

"We're across the face at the base of the second spire. Where are you?"

"Halfway across." I looked to my right and couldn't see Jack anymore, which meant he had rounded the corner. "Jack should almost be to you."

There was a hesitation, then he said, *"I see him. Are you okay?"*

"I'm good. I'm pulling hardware as I go."

"How's the ice?"

"Holding, but I don't know for how long."

"It's the same here. Your call, but I think we should start up this spire while we can."

"Go ahead."

"Zopa said he'll take the lead if it's okay with you."

Josh was going out of his way to let me know that I was in charge. This couldn't have been easy for him.

"Whatever you think is best."

"Okay, then." He sounded relieved. *"I'll start Zopa up. I'd guess it's six hundred meters to the top of the spire, then we'll have to drop down to the west and cross a glacier up to Camp Two."*

"Sounds good. I'll be along soon. I'll pull our protection as I work my way up behind you."

"If you think it's worth the risk."

"I'll bag it if I think it isn't."

"Good enough. Some of the screws this side of the face are old protection. I wouldn't waste my time trying to get them out. They're different from the anchors we're using. Part of the mountain now. I'd skip them."

"Good call. Thanks."

"I'll wait for Jack and have him climb ahead of me. Out."

I clipped the two-way to my harness, backed out the next screw, then moved to the next screw, which I could have pulled out with my fingertips. If I didn't hurry, the entire line was going to unzip with me on the end of it. I stopped using protection and free climbed just above the rope, pulling screws that came out easily and skipping the rest. By the time I reached the protection the Japanese had left behind, I was sweating. Josh was right; I wouldn't have been able to get them out with a jackhammer. By the time I got off the wall, the team was a third of the way up the next spire. Zopa was climbing fast, probably because of the temperature, which was now thirty-four degrees. Josh was lagging behind the team, no doubt waiting for me to catch up. I could see the summit of Hkakabo Razi looming a mile above, guarded by a half dozen jagged spires that looked impossible to climb.

"Peak?"

It was Josh. "I see you."

"It's getting a little soft up here. I wouldn't trust the protection. You should set your own. Don't bother pulling what Zopa set. We'll try to pop it out on our way back down."

"Roger that. I'll be right behind you. Keep moving. Out."

I had to slam my axes almost to the hilt to find ice solid enough to hold me. My crampons were of little use in the mush. The toe points were barely long enough to catch solid ice. Below was the glacier Hiro had tried to cross. It was totally impassable because of avalanche debris. If I didn't hurry, I would become a part of the debris. I paused to catch my breath and looked up. Josh was five hundred feet above me and hadn't moved an inch. I anchored myself and called him.

"Is there a problem?"

"No. I'm good here. It might be better if we climb together over this unstable ice. Cover each other's backs. You know what I mean? It's up to you. Over."

I wasn't sure it was up to me, at least not entirely. Josh was right. We should all be covering each other's backs on this treacherous ice. I shouldn't have slowed down to pull our protection. The "respectful climber" thing had put me at risk, and if Josh waited for me, it would put him at risk. I wanted to reassert my leadership role and tell him to catch up with the others, but that wasn't the right call.

"Thanks," I said. "I'll be right up."

As I climbed, I thought about something Mom had said before I left for Everest. I was complaining about Josh being a flake. She said, *When you're at the end of your rope, there is no one better than Joshua Wood. Unfortunately, he doesn't pay much attention until you're dangling.*

I wasn't exactly dangling, but climbing an unstable ice wall with unreliable protection could turn into a dangle at any second. Halfway up the wall, my right shoulder began to ache. I felt it weakening with every ax strike. The shoulder reminded me of Lwin. I wondered how Ethan was doing. Was he . . .

"Focus!" I shouted. "Get your head in the game."

The wind picked up, and with it a cold, damp fog. I glanced at my watch: 15,000 feet. Thirty degrees, temperature dropping, which was good.

"You still with us, Peak?"

I unclipped the radio. "I'm good. You can push on up. I'm going to start pulling anchors again." I didn't tell him that another reason for cleaning up was that it would slow me down and give my shoulder a rest.

"You sure?"

"Yeah. Head up to Camp Two. Out."

I tried to use my left arm as much as possible. This was helped by my toe points grabbing the ice, now that it was colder.

I finally reached the top of the spire—16,076 feet. Josh had not pushed on like I'd asked. He was sitting on the top, eating an energy bar. If I'd had the breath, I might have called him out for not heading up to Camp Two. Jack's drone was hovering five feet away, videotaping him eating. I sat down next to him on the craggy peak. The drone disappeared into the fog.

"I wish this was the summit and we were headed back down," Josh said.

I did too, but I could only nod because my breath was still ragged.

"While I was sitting here, I thought of another reason I wanted to climb Hkakabo Razi," he continued.

"What's that?" I managed to ask.

"I call it polarity, but that might not be the best word to describe it." He grinned. "And this might not be the best place to explain it."

"Give it a shot." My right shoulder was throbbing, and I needed another ten minutes to catch my breath before we made our way through the glacier three hundred feet below.

"This is how it works for me, and I didn't realize it until

I got to the top of this rock." Josh laughed. "Call it an alpine epiphany. Let's see if I can explain it. I think the reason I climb . . . the real reason . . . is because I'm good at it. I like the challenge, the simplicity, the quiet of climbing. But after a few weeks, I miss the noise, chaos, and confusion of civilization. These are the two poles I live between. When one pole goes bad, or gets boring, I flee to the opposite pole. Polarity. Yin yang the Taoists call it. I'm never satisfied at either pole, not for very long, anyway. When I got down from Everest, I was ecstatic with all of the attention . . . for about nine hours. That's when I decided to go on this climb. This doesn't exactly explain how I feel—it's all too new—but I know that it's true. Does it make any sense?"

"I'd have to think about it," I said, wondering if my taking over the lead on the climb had contributed to his dissatisfaction. I'd been thinking about that on the way up, not Josh's polarity, but the leadership part. I had no business leading this climb. I wasn't qualified. I didn't have enough experience. I looked at Josh. "I think I made a mistake saying I wanted to lead this climb."

Josh shook his head. "You didn't make a mistake. You're doing a good job. There's not one thing you've done that I wouldn't have done. No one has enough experience to lead a climb the first time they do it. It's a big responsibility with a lot of moving, or climbing, parts to manage. The only way you learn to lead a climb is to lead a climb."

"My shoulder is bothering me," I said.

"Explain."

I told him how it felt.

"I'll take a look at it. I'm pretty good with climbing injuries, having personally experienced hundreds of them over the years. And the aches and pains are coming more frequently the older I get."

"The reason I mention my shoulder is that I think you should take over the climb," I said.

"Nope. A bum shoulder is not a good enough reason. You're doing great. I'll let you know if you screw up."

"Like Mom did when I was young?"

Josh smiled. "Your mom always tells it like it is. It's a good quality, but sometimes it gets you in trouble."

"Have you ever talked about your polarity thing with Zopa?"

"If I did, he would just shrug."

I laughed.

"I'm serious. He's retired from climbing a dozen times that I know of. I bet he has the same polarity thing that I have. He checks into the monastery. It becomes monotonous. He checks out. He climbs a mountain. He checks back into the monastery."

I thought it was a little more complicated than that, but there was probably some truth to what Josh was saying. Zopa claimed that he climbed because he had to, not because he wanted to. I never quite bought this. I couldn't imagine Zopa not climbing.

"Is Zopa carrying a radio?"

"I think so."

I radioed him. He didn't answer.

"He's probably in the middle of something. He'll call back when he can." Josh looked at his watch. "Twenty-six degrees and falling. The longer we wait to drop down to the glacier, the safer we'll be from avalanche. I dumped my pack over the edge before you got here. Might as well dump yours too. We can rappel down. It'll save us a couple of hours of ice work. I've already rigged the lines."

I hadn't noticed the ropes hanging over the edge, or that he wasn't wearing a pack. It seemed to me that a climb leader should be more observant than this. Getting out of my pack was a huge relief. With it off, I felt like I was levitating above the spire. Josh lowered my pack over the edge while I tried to work the knot out of my shoulder. When he was done, he sat down behind me and started massaging my shoulder, which really hurt, but when he finished, it felt better.

The top of the spire was only about three feet square. Josh sat down next to me, let out a deep breath of frosty air, and looked at me. "I have something else I want to talk to you about. I know you've always been ticked about me not answering your letters."

"I'm over that. I've gotten used to our one-way corre-spondence." I wasn't exactly over it, but I was getting closer. "You don't have to write back. I don't expect you to write back. It's okay. It's not a priority. You're busy."

"That's not the problem, Peak. There's something you don't know. Something your mom hasn't told you."

I stared at him, wondering what was coming. Josh was as serious as I had ever seen him. Something Mom hadn't told me? We were very close. Until I was eight, it was just her and me in a little cabin in the Wyoming wilderness. What could this have to do with Josh not writing me back? Unless . . .

Something from my past resurfaced that hadn't haunted me for years. When I was nine years old, about the time I started sending Josh letters, I went through a period convinced that he wasn't my father like Mom had said. That some other guy, one she didn't want to talk about, was my father. I thought that Josh had agreed to take care of me and Mom from a distance because he and Mom had climbed together for years, breaking several speed records. When I asked Mom about this, she got mad. *Josh is your father! There's no more to this letter thing than the fact that Josh doesn't write. Let it go, Peak.*

"You look like you know what I'm going to say," Josh said.

"You're not my biological father," I said, before I could stop myself.

"Huh?" Josh looked shocked. "Did Teri . . . Did your mom tell you that?"

"No. I just thought—"

"I'm your dad. There's no doubt about it. This has nothing to do with that. It has to do with why I haven't written you back. You see . . ." He let out another long, foggy sigh. "You see . . . I can't read."

"What?" I couldn't have possibly heard him correctly. He had to be making some kind of weird joke that I didn't understand.

"Oh, I can figure out maps and some street signs," Josh continued. "But anything more complicated presents problems for me."

I hadn't heard wrong. This was more shocking to me than him not being my biological father.

"You've written several books and dozens of climbing articles," I said.

"I dictated the books and articles. I have someone transcribe the words onto paper. Someone reads me the edits. I respond to the edits verbally. Someone writes the corrections down, then I send the book or article back to the editor. Crazy, huh? Labor-intensive. Stupid."

"You're anything but stupid. You're brilliant and articulate. How did that happen without being able to read?"

He pointed at his ears. "I'm well listened. Books on tape and a good memory. When I was a kid, I learned to keep things in my brain because I couldn't take notes. I guess I have dyslexia or something. When I got older, I started using a digital recorder, which was a tremendous help."

I still couldn't wrap my mind around this. *There's no more to this letter thing than the fact that Josh doesn't write.* Mom hadn't lied to me, but she had come pretty close.

"No one knows?" I asked.

"A few people. Your mom knows and tried to help me when we were together, but it didn't stick. There's an entire ecosystem out there to help people like me, and it's gotten easier because of the Internet. If I want to listen to an article, it's an email and a few bucks away. Totally anonymous. They send me audio files of the articles I want, or need, to read. This is good and bad. Upside, people like me can stay informed. Downside, we don't do anything about our problem because we—at least the illiterates who have the money to pay for these services—don't have to."

No wonder Mom was such a fanatic with me about reading and writing when I was little. There was no television in our cabin. Just books.

"I didn't think it was a problem until you started to write me letters that I couldn't read. I was ashamed. I'm still ashamed. But I'm trying to do something about it. I hired a tutor in Chiang Mai. He's good, but the problem is that I'm rarely home. I've been too busy to address the problem, which is probably another reason I climb. Learning to read and write at my age is harder than summiting a mountain."

"I guess I should start sending you audible letters."

"Don't. You're the reason I'm going to learn how to read and write. Just don't make fun of me when you get a letter that looks like it's from a kindergartner."

"I won't. Thank you for telling me."

"If I'd known you were going to be so cool about it, I would have told you years ago."

"Peak?"

It was Zopa. "Go ahead."

"We just arrived at Camp Two. Five thousand one hundred meters. Where are you? Where is Josh?"

"We're together. We're just about ready to drop down to the glacier. How was the climb up to the camp?"

"A little soft, but it is getting colder now. There is a big snow-field above the glacier. You will have to cross below it. I saw no sign of it letting go, but I do not like how it looks. Best to hurry when you are beneath it."

"Thanks. We'll see you soon. Out."

Josh stood and stretched. "I feel better than I have in years, and I don't mean physically. A burden has been lifted. Now all I have to do is learn how to read and write. No worries."

"You'll do it. It's just another summit."

"Yep. And I can't fall and die."

The drone reappeared and hovered in front of us.

"Can Jack hear us?"

Josh shook his head. "I told him to switch the audio off." He pointed at the drone. "It is kind of irritating. I think we should call off the documentary."

"It hasn't been a problem so far."

"I'm calling it off."

I smiled. "Are you leading this climb?"

"Nope. Are you saying you want to be in it?"

"We'll see." A lot had changed in the ten minutes we had been on the top of the spire.

We dropped over the edge. The drone followed our slow descent to the glacier below.

TWENTY-FIVE

THE GLACIER WAS SCATTERED with blocks of ice as big as school buses. Josh was ten feet away from me coiling the ropes. I could barely see him through the fog. The wind had completely stopped. The only sound was cracking and shifting ice, which was not unusual on a glacier, but unnerving with the threat of avalanche.

"It's a little weird out," Josh said, tying up the last rope.

"That's an understatement."

I slipped into my pack and winced.

"You okay?"

"Sort of," I said, trying to find the sweet spot for my right strap. It turned out there wasn't a sweet spot, just less-sour spots.

"Peak?"

Zopa again. "Go ahead."

"Are you on the glacier?"

"We just rappelled down."

"How is it?"

"Fog. Terrible visibility. No wind."

"Do you know where you are?"

"I think so, but it's hard to be certain without any land-marks."

"I have provided landmarks."

"Come again?"

"Ice marks. Saffron."

I looked at Josh. "Do you know what he's talking about?"

Josh shook his head.

"Bread crumbs."

"Ah," Josh said, pointing.

Three feet in front of us was a strip of saffron cloth stuck to the block of ice. We walked over to it. Zopa had cut off pieces of his robe to guide us.

"Got it," I said.

"It is a maze. Move quickly. The air is warming."

"Roger that. Out."

"Twenty-nine degrees," Josh said.

"Let's go."

We zigzagged our way through the frozen labyrinth. It was like I was wandering through a dream with my father and remnants of Zopa in the form of strips of saffron cloth cling-ing to the ice like limp prayer flags. If it hadn't been for the tracks, we would have never found Zopa's bread crumbs. In a few places Zopa had taken a wrong turn and had to backtrack. In other places there was no way forward except to climb up and over a humungous ice block.

"How far are you?"

Josh and I had just topped an ice block, and I was descending. I didn't have a free hand to answer. Josh had already reached the bottom and took the call.

"Not sure. It's slow going in the fog."

"How many flags have you passed?"

"I have no idea."

Josh looked up at me. I shook my head. I didn't know either. It hadn't occurred to me to count them.

"I placed twelve of them."

If we had counted, as Zopa had obviously hoped, we would have known how far away we were.

"Was it clear when you went through here?" Josh asked.

"Yes. But I knew the fog was coming. This is why I made the flags."

I dropped down next to Josh. The next flag was about ten feet from us. I could barely see it through the fog. Visibility was a little better, but not by much.

"The flags are different lengths. Shorter at the beginning. Longer where you will climb up to camp."

"Thanks," Josh said. "We need to get moving. Out." He looked at me. "Did you notice the different lengths?"

"I noticed, but I didn't know what they meant."

"Me either. I think we should have let Zopa lead this climb."

"I think he is leading this climb."

"Ha. Good point. I get the same feeling every time I climb with him. He knew the fog was coming long before the fog knew it was coming. The guy's a weather guru. I've known him for twenty years. He has never been wrong about the weather."

The cloth strip, or flag, as Zopa called it, was about seven inches long. The next one was eight or nine inches long. I radioed Zopa.

"How long is the last flag?"

"One foot. Maybe a little longer."

"We're three or four inches from that one." I wished it was literally only three or four inches.

"What is the temperature?"

I looked at my watch, wishing I hadn't. "Thirty-three."

"Thirty-five up here. Move quickly. Out."

We had four, or five, flags before we reached Camp Two, and no idea of how far away it was. We moved quickly, as Zopa suggested, without a word between us. Sometimes I took the lead, sometimes Josh took the lead as we scurried over and zigzagged through the frozen obstacle course. At the eleventh flag, there was a loud crack followed by a deafening roar to our right.

"Dump your pack!" Josh shouted. "Run!"

We ran parallel to the terrifying sound. You can't outrun an avalanche. All you can do is get as close to the edge as you can before it mows you down. I felt a cold blast of wind. Josh grabbed me by the shoulder and turned me into the wall of snow and ice.

"Climb it!" he shouted. "Swim up!"

The white wall smacked into me.

Everything went black.

TWENTY-SIX

PITCH-DARK.

I couldn't tell if my eyes were open or closed.

I couldn't tell if I was upside down or right side up.

I'd read a lot about avalanches and had taken a couple avalanche courses, but this was the first one I'd ever been in. It was much worse than I had imagined. I'd been taught not to think about panic phrases like *buried alive* or *icy grave*, or words like *suffocation* and *asphyxia*, which were exactly the phrases and words running through my brain. My right arm was pinned to my side. My left hand was in front of my face. I could wiggle my fingers, barely. I could turn my head from side to side, barely. I could breathe, barely, which meant that there was a little air in my *icy grave*. But for how long? I could not feel my legs. In fact, it felt like I didn't have legs, or feet, or a torso, or . . . Where was Josh? He'd let go of my shoulder an instant before the wall hit us. He needed both arms to swim, or "climb" the wave. Bizarre, I know. The theory is that the higher you can go, the shallower you'll be buried. You are supposed to carry a location beacon and turn it on, so someone can find you. My location beacon was in my bedroom closet in New York. I hadn't thought I'd need it in Burma. Weirdly, Ethan hadn't packed one either in all the junk he had been hauling around. I wondered how Ethan was doing. I hoped he was doing better than me . . .

Focus, Peak! I told myself.

What did I have in my pockets? This was another technique they taught in avalanche class. Ask yourself questions to keep your mind off suffocating to death, reducing your panic, thereby conserving oxygen.

I was wearing cargo pants. I had a lot of pockets to contemplate. My wallet and passport were buttoned in my back pocket. They would be able to identify me if I was ever found. I had a multitool knife in my right front cargo pocket. In the regular pocket above that were two energy bars, one of them half eaten. The sat phone was in my left cargo pocket. Useless because it wouldn't work underground. Even if it did, I couldn't reach it. Ethan's spoon was also in my left pocket. This made me smile. I almost laughed. Buried alive, and my only hope was Ethan's treasured spoon. But could I wiggle my arm down to the pocket and retrieve it?

It wasn't easy. I had to dig my way down to the pocket, which helped me by widening the space I was stuck in. The instructor's words came back to me. *You must do something to save yourself! You are not an ice cube waiting to be dropped into a drink, or a grave. You are a living human being.* She had survived two avalanches. In the second, she had been buried for nearly twenty-four hours. I found the spoon handle and was able to inch it out by pinching it between my index and middle fingers. I slowly brought it up and started chipping away at the ice above my head. I wasn't sure, but I thought I was on my back because ice and snow were falling on my face. The only thing that could cause that was gravity. My body heat was melting the snow and ice, but not enough to move my right arm. It would have been handy to have my knife to help with the chipping. I worked slowly, not making a lot of progress, but at least I was trying to do something to save myself. Hypothermia would be the next problem. I was bundled up pretty well, layered, but my clothes were soaked with ice water now. As I chipped away, I repeated the litany I had learned from the same woman who had taught me about avalanche survival. We had to know it verbatim and had to repeat it in order anytime she randomly commanded us. *Shivering comes in waves. Violently pauses. The pauses get longer until the shivering finally ceases because the heat output from burning glycogen in the muscles is not sufficient to counteract the continually dropping core temperature. The shivering stops to conserve glucose. Muscle rigidity develops because peripheral blood flow is . . .*

I was at number one. Shivering, but not too violently, yet. *Scrape . . .*

A large chunk of snow, or ice, hit me in the face, making me sputter, but I couldn't have been happier about it. I was digging myself out a spoonful at a time. In another couple of feet, I might be able to sit up. *Scrape . . .*

We probably shouldn't have dumped our packs. I had trekking and tent poles I could have used to pop through the top, to say nothing about my ice axes, which would have eaten through the snow and ice in minutes. But if we hadn't dumped our gear, we would have been hit by the center mass of the avalanche, which would have buried us under thirty feet of snow.

Us.

I hoped Josh was still with me. *Scrape* . . .

We were just getting to know each other. *Scrape* . . .

Not being able to read or write, then having to hide it, must have been a nightmare for him. *Scrape* . . .

I started shivering. Semiviolently. The good news was that my body had melted the ice enough for me to move my right arm. I slipped my hand into my pocket and pulled out my knife. I was in the process of choosing the right chipping blade when I realized I could actually see the knife, not clearly, but enough to see that it was a knife, which meant that I had spooned my way to the light, dim but luminescent. I started chipping away, spoon in one hand, knife pliers in the other, ignoring my shivers, lack of oxygen, and fast-approaching hypothermia.

My hole got lighter with every desperate scrape. Finally, I broke through the surface. I put my face as close to the tiny opening as I could and took in a lungful of fresh air. I was considerably weaker than when I started, but the light and the air inspired me to keep going. *Scrape* . . . *scrape* . . . *scrape* . . . *scrape*—

Josh's bearded face suddenly appeared in the small opening. "Over here!" he shouted. "Steady. We'll get you out. I thought I lost you." There were tears running down his face.

Zopa appeared above the hole. "Cover your face."

He widened the hole with an ice ax. I don't remember being pulled out, but I do remember being stripped naked, dried off, and enough fragmented sentences to put together what had happened. When the wave hit us, unlike me, Josh had an ice ax in his hand. He was buried, but dug himself out within a few minutes. He called and called for me. Zopa and the brothers rappelled down from Camp Two and joined the search. Jack launched his drone from camp and did a grid search. He didn't find me, but he located our packs, or what was left of them. They searched in complete silence so they could hear my call . . . if I was still alive. Josh was a foot away from me when he heard me chipping away with my knife and Ethan's spoon.

"Lucky," Josh said.

"Karma," Zopa said.

Freezing cold, I thought, shivering in my dry clothes all the way up to Camp Two, helped along by Josh and Zopa because my frozen arms and legs weren't working well. They half carried me into the green tent, wrapped me in my sleeping bag, and gave me mug after mug of scalding hot tea. It took an hour for me to stop shivering and comprehend the quiet conversations around me, the fact that the sun had set, and that the wind was howling outside. I think the only reason the tent didn't blow away was because our entire team and all of our gear were crammed inside. There was barely enough room to scratch yourself.

"What's happening?" I asked.

"He speaks!" Josh said. "Can you feel your arms and legs?"

"Yes. They're sore."

"That's good." He pulled out a bottle of aspirin from his pack and shook out three for me to down.

I looked at my watch. It was ten p.m. I'd been in a semi-conscious stupor for nearly five hours. I swallowed the aspirin and washed them down with tea.

"More tea?" Yash asked.

I shook my head. I needed to get outside before my bladder burst. Josh helped me through the flap and held me by the belt so I didn't get blown off the mountain while I peed for what felt like an hour. Back inside, I wolfed down a mug of beef stew, after which I felt almost human.

"Thanks, everyone, for saving me," I said.

"You were close to saving yourself," Zopa said.

I looked at Josh. "I'm glad you made it out. I was worried."

He grinned. "I can't die now. I have important things to learn."

I returned the grin. "That's right. So what's our situation?"

"We're kind of stuck," Josh said. "The fog cleared out just before dark. The avalanches hammered the glacier."

"Avalanches?"

"There were two more. One as we were climbing up here, and one an hour after we got into the tent. I don't think you'd come around enough to hear either of them."

I nodded. I hadn't seen or heard anything while I thawed out. I thought about the next stage of the climb. With luck, we'd be up on the ridge at Camp Three by tomorrow afternoon, well above any avalanche threat.

"What do you mean by stuck?"

"We cannot go back down the way we came up," Zopa said. "It is blocked."

He couldn't possibly know this for certain. "There must be a way through," I said.

"Perhaps, but it could take days to find it."

"Not enough supplies," Yash said.

"Not enough food," Yogi clarified.

"How many days of food do we have?" I asked.

Jack spoke up for the first time. "Your and Josh's backpacks were shredded by the avalanche. Most of your equipment and clothes survived, but every scrap of food you were hauling was ruined."

"We have enough food for six or seven days," Josh said. "Which would have been plenty if we'd been able to return along the same route. Two days to reach the summit and three days back, weather permitting. We could save two days by aborting right here and using those extra days to figure a way through the blocked glacier. But there's no guarantee we'll make it through. We could be bumping around the glacier for a month and not find a way out."

"Do we still have my sketches?" I asked. They were in the journal the twins had given me.

Jack started rummaging through a loose pile of clothes and gear. We were going to have to figure out how to carry the junk without packs.

"This?" Jack held up my journal.

"That's it."

He handed it to me. I turned to the back pages where I had my Hkakabo Razi notes. Everything was intact. The twins were going to get a kick out of their journal being water- and avalanche-proof, if I ever saw them again. I laid the journal on the floor near the lantern, then flipped through the pages with everyone looking on. The sketches were crude, but good enough for me to visualize the photos and videos that had inspired them.

I pointed to the ridge. "This is as far as Hiro and his team got, a little over seventeen thousand feet. Our Camp Three. They ran into bad weather and a supply problem, and had to turn back."

"Gotta know when to turn back," Josh said.

"But in our case, we cannot turn back," Zopa said. "Not along the same route we have traveled to get here."

"There's a ridge midway between Camp Three and the summit," I continued. "If we follow it south, we'll be safe from avalanches. There are some high spires along it, but we might be able to traverse them if the snow and ice look solid. I think it would save us a day, or maybe two. Chin might be able to pick us up at the bottom, or drop enough food for us to get to a safe landing zone."

"Assuming that this Chin is willing to fly his helicopter over here," Josh said.

"He will come," Zopa said.

I hadn't told Josh about Zopa saving Chin's life, and *changing* Chin's life.

Josh grinned. "I take that as gospel."

"So, we'll see what the weather is like tomorrow," I said. "If it's good, we climb up to Camp Three. If the weather is bad, we'll take another look at our options. Sound okay?"

Five exhausted heads nodded.

"Did my tent make it?" I asked.

"Yeah," Jack said. "And Josh's."

"But we're all sleeping in here tonight," Josh said.

"There's not a lot of real estate outside. It'll be warmer with all of us inside, and we'll be able to break camp quicker tomorrow morning."

We climbed into our sleeping bags, side by side, head to toe, like sardines. I chose the outside wall where it would be cooler. I rolled onto my side and felt something jamming into my thigh. Sat phone. I'm ashamed to say that I had completely forgotten about Ethan. I pulled it out and turned it on. There were two voice messages from Alessia.

"Peak. Ethan has gone into surgery for what they call a decompressive craniectomy, or DC. The doctors will remove a piece of his skull until his brain swelling has diminished, then they will replace the piece of skull. He has been put into an induced coma because he is so agitated. I called his sister in the United States. She is flying into Yangon tomorrow. She will be a guest of the embassy. My mother arrived this morning. She was unhappy about Hkakabo Razi, but hopes you are safe and reach the summit. The last thing Ethan said before they put him into a coma was that he wanted his spoon."

I stifled a laugh. I was looking forward to telling him that his spoon had saved my life. I played the second message.

"Peak. I know you are climbing, but I hope you receive this. Ethan is out of surgery. According to the doctors, he is doing well, but I think he looks terrible. They say that is normal. They were able to stop the bleeding. As soon as the swelling goes down, they will replace the piece of skull. His sister is here, and she is very nice. She says that she was able to buy her mother's silverware set back from the woman who bought it. She too wants that spoon. Climb safe."

I closed my eyes with the cold wind beating against the tent and a smile on my face.

TWENTY-SEVEN

I WAS AWAKE AS THE FIRST RAY OF SUN came through the tent. It felt good to be alive. I stayed still so I wouldn't disturb anyone. It wasn't long before the others started stirring. Yogi lit the stove as Yash sorted through our reduced food supply. I got up, carefully stepped over Josh, Zopa, and Jack, and went outside.

The sun was just coming up behind Hkakabo Razi. A small disk-shaped cloud covered the summit. It was the only cloud in the dark blue sky. There was a slight wind, and it was twenty-one degrees out. Perfect climbing weather. Josh wasn't kidding about there not being much real estate outside the tent. It was a three-foot step to death. No wonder Josh had held on to my belt while I peed the night before. Zopa was right about the glacier too. It was an unstable, jumbled mess.

Zopa came out and stood next to me, surveying the problem. "How do you feel today?"

I hadn't given a thought to how I felt, which meant I must have felt pretty good. "I'm ready to climb."

We turned around and looked at the north ridge. Four hundred feet above us, steep, but smooth enough to pull our gear up behind us without hauling it on our backs.

"Easy," Zopa said.

IT WAS EASY. We were on the ridge before eight o'clock. The weather held. We had redistributed the gear into three packs. It would have been four packs, but Jack had enough equipment in his pack to film a television series and there was no room. We hauled the packs up to the ridge, which was about eighteen inches wide. Hiro had said it ranged from six inches to four feet wide. Camp Three was a semiflat area about ten feet square at about 18,000 feet. Beyond that, there was virtually no information about the climb up to the summit. I decided to set up two three-man teams. I'd lead the first team with Yash in the middle and Zopa at the end. The second team would be Josh in the lead followed by Jack and Yogi. The lead climbers would not carry backpacks, but we'd switch off lead duty throughout the day to give the packers a rest. We would travel roped together. This would give us a chance to belay anyone who slipped off.

I moved out slowly, feeling my way forward with alpine trekking poles.

Tap . . . tap . . . tap . . . step . . . tap . . . tap . . . tap . . .

The footing was treacherous, but I'd been on worse ridges on Everest and McKinley. The wind picked up a little, but the sky remained clear. About halfway up to the first col, I heard a loud thump and dropped to my knees. I glanced behind. My team and Josh's had done the same. An avalanche had let loose on the northern side, nearly shaking us off the ridge. The best, and safest, way to see an avalanche is from above, and we had a beautiful view. Jack was straddling the ridge, filming it. He got up to his knees to get a better shot and fell over the edge. Josh and Yogi saw it immediately and caught him before he cratered. I waited until they got him back up to the ridge to call.

"Is he okay?" I asked.

"A couple scrapes," Josh said. *"Nothing serious."*

"I think we need to skip filming while we're on this ridge."

"Roger that. I already told him."

"Are we good to go?"

"Yep. I'll give him a couple of minutes to catch his breath. We'll be right behind you. Magnificent avalanche, wasn't it?"

"Beautiful. Did he catch any of it?"

"He's nodding."

"Good. I look forward to seeing it." The avalanche was already permanently burned into my brain. I didn't need to see it again, but I didn't want Jack to feel bad for making such a boneheaded mistake. I knew how that felt.

Before I got back to my feet, I asked Zopa and Yash if they wanted to switch with me. "I'm happy to take a turn with a pack. My shoulder's feeling good. I'm feeling strong." They both shook their heads.

Tap . . . tap . . . tap . . . step . . . tap . . . tap . . . tap . . .

We reached the top of the first spire at 17,716 feet. I stopped to check on Josh before we started down to the col, where we would lose sight of them for a while. They were about a hundred yards behind, climbing steadily.

Walking downhill on ice is always harder than walking uphill. I slipped several times, but managed to catch myself with my poles before I plunged over the side. We rested on the col while we waited for Josh's team to top the spire and start down.

"Let me take one of the packs."

Zopa shook his head. "I'll let you know when I want to switch."

Yash said something in Nepalese that I didn't understand.

Zopa laughed. "He says that he is fine too. He gave Yogi the heavier pack."

Yash pointed to the top of our next spire and said something else. Hiro's camp was supposed to be two thirds of the way up.

"He wants to know if you want to fix ropes up to the camp. He says it will be easier to get up the hill."

"I want Yash to fix ropes up to top, and I'll carry the pack since it's so light."

Zopa translated. Yash laughed and nodded. It was a fair exchange. Yash and Yogi were probably the best in the world at fixing ropes ahead of climbing expeditions. They had done it their entire lives. He grabbed a couple coils of rope and a bag of hardware, and started up the ridge like a mountain goat.

I started to put on his pack, but Zopa stopped me. "Might as well wait here for him to finish. It will be safer."

I was more than happy to wait. I pulled the sat phone out and turned it on. There was a message from Alessia that was less than ten minutes old.

"*Peak. Good morning. Ethan looks better, but of course he is still in a coma. The doctors are hopeful. They plan to bring him out of the coma soon. I hope you are getting these messages. Please say hello to Zopa for me.*"

This is when I realized I hadn't told Alessia that Josh, Jack, Yogi, and Yash were climbing with us, that I hadn't talked to her since Zopa had been leading me to a base camp that I didn't know existed. I called her, intending to leave a voice message, but she answered.

"*Peak.*"

"It's good to hear your voice. How are you? How's Ethan?"

"*As good as can be expected. Where are you?*"

"Sitting on a col with Zopa at close to eighteen thousand feet. We'll reach Camp Three on the next pitch. It's a beautiful day. I wish you were here. I wish Ethan was here."

"*I do too.*"

"I'll have to keep this short to conserve the sat battery, but I wanted to tell you that we have a six-member team. Zopa invited some old friends to climb with us. Yogi and Yash —brothers, Sherpas—that I climbed with on Everest. Jack from JR's video team—"

"*Jack is there!*"

"Yes."

"*How is he?*"

"Good. He's climbing well. He's fit."

"*I so wish I was there!*"

"And one more person. My father, Joshua Wood."

"*He is there?*"

"Yes."

"But he just finished the seven summits. I thought that he was at his home in Thailand."

"No one knows he's here."

"Now I am very jealous."

"I didn't tell you this to make you jealous. I just wanted you to know that it's not just Zopa and me climbing."

"It is a relief. Even my mother was worried about you and Zopa climbing Hkakabo Razi alone. She spoke to your mother on the phone."

I would like to have heard that conversation. "You might want to call her yourself and tell her who I'm climbing with. That will make her feel better."

"Yes, and I will give her your phone number."

"I probably won't be able to answer, but okay."

"Is Jack filming the climb?"

"Kind of."

"You did not want the climb filmed."

"No. I have a lot to tell you when I see you."

"But you are all right. The climb is going well?"

"Not exactly. We're kind of in a pickle."

"A pickle?"

"A jam . . . a slight problem. Avalanches. We can't climb down the same way we climbed up. We haven't figured out a return route yet, and we're a bit low on food. Can you call Chin and tell him that we might need his help in the next few days?"

"Certainly, but—"

"We're fine." Josh's team had just reached the col. "Look,

I better go. We have to get up to Camp Three while the weather is good. I'll be in touch. I miss you." I ended the call, got up, and made my way over to Jack. "Are you okay?"

He gave me a sheepish smile. "Just embarrassed. It was a stupid move."

"That's okay. Just glad you didn't crater."

"Fixed ropes, huh?" Josh said, looking at Yash's handiwork.

Yash was already halfway up the pitch, slamming in hardware with barely a pause.

"We'll wait until Yash gets to the camp," I said.

"At the rate he's going, it won't be long." Josh sat down next to me. "If we were just a little closer, we could try for the summit today."

Josh was right. The weather was perfect for a summit attempt, but we weren't nearly close enough. It was one o'clock. "Even with the fixed ropes, we won't reach camp until three," I said.

Josh glanced at his watch. "At the earliest."

We ate a little food, hydrated, and waited. The radio crackled. Yash said something in Nepalese, which Josh understood, adding to my shock that he couldn't read or write.

"He's at camp. He's going to anchor the rope and wants to know if you want him to continue up to see what's over the next peak. He says that he has plenty of rope left over. He'll fix as much as he has, which will save us a lot of time tomorrow."

"What do you think?"

"The weather is good right now. Take advantage of it while you can. Who knows what the weather will be like tomorrow."

Both of us looked at Zopa, who shrugged, then looked up at the sky. After about a minute, he said, "More wind, but clear tomorrow."

I keyed the radio. "Fix more rope."

"Good," Yash said.

TWENTY-EIGHT

THE PITCH WAS LONG AND THE RIDGE NARROW, but there was little danger because we were clipped onto the fixed ropes. We reached Camp Three at 3:02. I think Yash had been kidding about the weight of his pack. It weighed a ton. I was happy to get it off my back. The site was only marginally bigger than the previous camp. There was room for the green tent and maybe a couple small tents. At least we wouldn't be packed in like we had been the night before. We retrieved the ropes behind us. The only signs of Yash were the ropes he had fixed up the next pitch. I gave him a call on the two-way.

"Yash?"

"Okay."

"Where are you?"

Yash answered in Nepalese.

"He is on a col between the spire above us and the next spire," Zopa translated. "He's fixed all of the rope that he has."

I handed the radio to Zopa. "No point in me asking questions if I can't understand the answers."

"The brothers can both speak English," Zopa said. "But sometimes they prefer not to." He spoke into the radio for a while. Yash responded, again preferring not to speak English.

"He says that he is on a col near the place you thought we might be able to climb down. The site is flatter and larger than our camp. He thinks we could reach it in less than two hours."

I asked Jack if he could launch the drone and show us what Yash was talking about.

"Sure thing!" He started assembling his gear.

For someone who was antigizmo, I was certainly taking advantage of the technology. We gathered around the tablet and watched the flight. Jack flew the drone along the side of the ridge, not over the top, so he didn't lose contact with the machine. The images were beautiful. When he reached the col, Yash waved at us. He was right; the col was twice as big as our camp, and of course, closer to the summit.

"What does everyone think?"

"Plenty of light," Josh said. "Shouldn't be too hard with fixed ropes."

I looked at Zopa. "Better campsite and closer to your route down. It would be best to see it before we try for the summit."

"Yogi, Jack, any opinion?"

Yogi said something. Josh and Zopa laughed.

Josh interpreted. "He says Yash only wants to camp there

because he doesn't want to come back and carry the heavy pack."

"I thought his pack was heavier than Yash's."

Yogi chose to respond in English. "I took ten pounds from my pack. Put it into his pack. He wasn't looking."

Which meant I'd been carrying the heaviest pack.

"I say we go for it," Jack said.

WE REACHED YASH'S COL just before dark. He had spent his long wait smoothing out a level area about fifteen feet square. We could see my escape route in the waning light. It looked terribly dangerous. A huge avalanche let loose while we were looking.

"Maybe the shadows are making it look more ominous than it actually is," Josh said. I think he was trying to make me feel better. It didn't work. I had led my team into a dead end. I knew it. We all knew it. We ate very little at dinner, saying we were full, which was a lie. We had burnt thousands of calories that day. I was hungry enough to eat my boots. So was everyone else. The brothers set up the green tent in the middle with four small tents around it. They said they would sleep in the big tent so they could wake up and get breakfast prepared for an early start.

"Yeah," Jack said. "But which way are we going?"

He wasn't being a jerk. He was just voicing what we were all thinking.

For an hour we discussed aborting the summit attempt and taking our chances on the glacier. The thinking was that if we left at first light and ditched some of our gear, we might be able to get down to the glacier in one horrendous day.

For the next half hour, we discussed the possibility of Chin picking us up off the mountain. Helicopters could certainly land at 18,000 feet. In 2005, Didier Delsalle, a French helicopter pilot, landed on the top of Everest, 29,030 feet. He tried to do it again the following day and wasn't able to complete the landing. No one has ever tried it again. But the problem with Hkakabo Razi was not the altitude; it was that there was nowhere to land, which led us back to the tumbled glacier. If we failed, we could call in the Burmese army to rescue us by hovering and roping up to the cockpit. I was certain that Alessia's mother could, and would, arrange a rescue with the government if we needed it.

"So we're not going to die out here," Jack said, with some relief.

"That depends," Zopa said. "A helicopter is useless if the weather is bad."

These were the first words he had spoken since we started the discussion.

"Is the weather going to get bad?" Josh asked.

Zopa nodded. "Very bad. Not tomorrow, but the day after on this side of the mountain, and it will last for several days. The south side will be relatively clear. Our descent should be into Tibet."

"The plateau?" Josh asked.

Zopa nodded again.

The Tibetan Plateau is the largest and highest plateau in the world, covering nearly a million square miles.

"We drop down from here?" I asked.

Zopa shook his head. "It would be a shame to come all this way and not summit. We can top the mountain, then drop down onto the roof of the world."

TWENTY-NINE

JOSH WAS ALREADY UP DRINKING TEA when I walked into the green tent. It was still dark, with millions of stars in the clear sky. It was fifteen degrees out, and the wind had picked up as Zopa had predicted. I had slept well after I stopped worrying about the roof of the world.

"Beautiful day to summit," Josh said cheerfully.

Yash poured me a mug of tea.

"What do you think of Zopa's plan?" I asked.

"It's just as viable as our other choices, none of which are good. How about you and me heading out before the others and fixing some ropes?"

I asked Yogi and Yash what they thought of the idea. They both gave a Zopa shrug, then Yash said, "Go light. We will carry the packs." Yogi nodded in agreement.

Twenty minutes later, Josh and I were headed up a steep pitch, loaded down with rope and hardware, wearing headlamps on our foreheads and crampons on our boots. We took turns with the lead, the person in front fixing the rope and the person behind checking protection. We didn't talk. We didn't have time. But we did pause an hour after we started to watch the sun peek out from behind Hkakabo Razi.

I think that was the point that summit fever set in. At least for me. Josh too, judging by the speed he was climbing. The top looked close enough to reach out and touch. This is the sweet spot in climbing, when every thought, worry, and dread disappears. It's also the time when you make mistakes.

I fell over the edge while I was clipping into the rope. Josh's hand reached out and grabbed me by my wrist. The only thing between me and death was his strength. *When you're at the end of your rope, there is no one better than Joshua Wood. Unfortunately, he doesn't pay much attention until you're dangling.* I had Josh's complete attention, but he was slipping off the ridge.

"Let me go."

He shook his head.

From where I was dangling, I couldn't tell if he was clipped in or not. "No use in us both going over."

"I'm not letting you die alone! Try! Save me!"

He meant it. If I didn't find a way to save myself, he was going down with me. He closed his eyes and focused on being my anchor. I saw the pain and strain in his face. I had my ice ax in my free hand. The wall was three feet away from me. I was going to have to swing toward it and try to plant my ax. I had one shot at this. Josh didn't have the strength for a second swing.

"Hang tight!" I shouted, and swung. The ax slipped a fraction of an inch, then caught. I buried my toe points into the ice. "I'm good! Let go!"

Josh opened his eyes and looked down at me, making sure I wasn't saving him by falling.

"You're sure."

I nodded.

He let my wrist go. I pulled myself into the wall.

Josh disappeared. A few seconds later, a rope came over the edge and slapped me in the back. I managed to hook it into my harness. Josh took up the tension.

"I've got you!" he shouted from the ridge. I couldn't see him. "Come on up!"

I climbed. When I reached the edge of the ridge, I saw Josh lying on his back, belaying me with the rope through his harness. I pulled myself over the edge and sat down next to him, gasping for breath.

"Thanks," I said as soon as I could get the word out.

Josh sat up. "That was damn close. Did you really think that I would drop you?"

"I'm glad you didn't, but it seemed like the best solution at the time."

"For the record, I might not return your letters, or be around very much, but I would never drop you. What happened?"

"I fixed the rope and slipped before I clipped in."

Josh nodded. "You take the lead. Let's get to the top."

I moved slowly, with deliberation, my summit fever gone, or at least diminished. Zopa radioed that they were on their way up. We switched the lead back and forth several more times. I stopped a hundred feet from the top and waited for Josh.

"What's the problem?" he asked when he caught up to me.

"No problem. I want you to take the lead."

"This close to the summit? Forget it."

"My climb."

"Then climb. You need to be the first to the top, if for no other reason than for your real teammates, who couldn't be here. I'll be right behind you."

I reached the summit half an hour later. The wind was blowing fifty miles an hour. It was 12:35 p.m. The sky was clear above the mountain, but I could see dark, ominous clouds to the south, coming our way. Josh pulled himself up, sat down next to me, and gave me a high-five. He reached into his pocket and pulled out a certified GPS unit. I hadn't even looked at my watch to see how high I was perched. It didn't matter. We had made it to the top.

"Any guesses?" Josh asked.

"All I know is that you can see everything from up here." I pointed to the Tibetan Plateau far below. "The climb down looks pretty straightforward. I guess we aren't going to starve or freeze to death."

"Zopa," Josh said, shaking his head. "He always finds a way."

He switched the GPS on and looked at the screen.

"Do you want to know?"

I thought about this for a few moments. I did and I didn't want to know. It was kind of cool to think there was still a mountain without an official elevation. A mystery. But everyone was going to know soon enough.

"Tell me," I said.

"We're on the highest mountain in Southeast Asia. Gamlang Razi is 19,259 feet. Hkakabo Razi is 19,643 feet, give or take a foot or two."

I called Alessia.

"We're at the summit."

"I am so happy! Is it the tallest?"

"Yes. How's Ethan?"

"The swelling went down, and they put him back together again. I am in his room right now. I will put the phone on speaker. He is groggy, but awake." There was some noise, then Alessia came back on. *"It is Peak."*

"Are you on the summit?" Ethan asked.

"Yep. A beautiful day at nineteen-thousand-six-hundred-and-forty-three feet."

"Perfect." Ethan's voice was weak, but clear.

"How are you doing?"

"I have a headache."

"I bet. Are you there, Alessia?"

"Yes, I am here."

"Did you talk to Chin?"

"He said that he would help you in any way he could. He is flying back to Strangeland, so he is nearby."

"Tell him we aren't going back to Burma. We are climbing down to the Tibetan Plateau. We'll be down in a few days. Looks like an easy descent from where I'm sitting. I'm not sure if we'll need him. Tell him I'll keep him posted on our progress if the battery holds out." I glanced at the battery icon. It was low.

"Your mother said that she left you a message."

I looked at the screen. There was a message. "I don't

have much battery left. Can you call her and tell her that we're okay? I'll call her as soon as I can, but it might be a few days."

"Of course."

"I better cut this off. I'll call you from Tibet. I'm glad you're better, Ethan."

"Me too. What about my spoon?"

"Your spoon saved my life. I'll tell you about it when I see you." I turned the sat phone off.

The drone appeared. Josh held the GPS up to it.

"Are you going to be in the documentary?"

"Looks like I'm already in it." I smiled and waved at the camera.

I put my arm around my dad and gave him a hug. "Thanks for coming."

He returned the hug and said, "No worries."

I smiled. I think that phrase is Josh's version of Zopa's shrug.

Yash, Yogi, Jack, and Zopa joined us on the summit. We sat there taking in the magnificent view for several minutes without a word.

"I guess we should start down," I said.

"Who will lead?" Zopa asked.

"I led us up here," I said. "I think you should lead us down."

Zopa shrugged and began the long climb down.

Acknowledgments

There are a lot more people behind this novel than the lowly author. My heartfelt thanks go to the wonderful HMH team: Catherine Onder, Mary Magrisso, Cara Llewellyn, Jim Secula, Amanda Acevedo, Diane Varone, and my new climbing partner and editor, Lily Kessinger. I would also like to thank my longtime agent, Barbara Kouts, who has blazed my book trail for over two decades. No acknowledgments would be complete without my dear wife, Marie, who does more for my books, and me, than anyone will ever know.

5.18